THE MONSTER MAKER

Books by Bill Willingham
published by Clockwork Storybook

Down the Mysterly River

The Beowulf Series:

The Monster Maker

Hyde & Seek

THE
MONSTER
MAKER

Bill Willingham

The Monster Maker

Clockwork Storybook, Inc.
P.O. Box 200126
Austin, TX 78720
comments@clockworkstorybook.com

ISBN: 0-9704841-8-6

Printed in the United States of America

**To my friend, Mike Sinner
real live action figure**

A Short Note Before We Begin

This story – and the Beowulf stories that will follow in subsequent books – takes place in my fictional world of Coventry, which was originally created for my short lived (so far) comic book series of the same name. The series was written and illustrated by me, published by Fantagraphics Books, and all three issues are still available from your local comics shop, or directly from the publisher (the ordering information for those comics can be found on the last page of this book).

The Coventry of the title is an imagined 51st state – located on the United States' west coast, south of Washington and north of Oregon – and Pandora is its largest city.

The main character of this story appeared in two out of the three issues of Coventry, the comic book series, but those books shouldn't be required to make sense of this tale.

And that's all I'm going to tell you for now.

Chapter One
Death in the Mountains

Seventeen years earlier Robert Olney had walked out on Kathy, his live-in girlfriend, following their third fight in as many days. As usual she'd mentioned marriage and he'd mentioned abortion. Afterwards the verbal clawing and slashing followed more or less along the established lines of their often-rehearsed script. Robert packed a single bag while Kathy ineffectually tried to pull it out of his hands or pin his arms, all the while begging him to stay. She wept loudly as he left, sitting on the dull golden colored shag carpet of their one-room apartment, rocking back and forth, cradling her growing belly in her arms.

Now in his new home, far away from Kathy in both distance and time, Robert looked again at the single Polaroid photograph that had arrived in a letter to him nine days ago, when the road from Grant had last been clear enough for the mail to get through. It was a picture of a young and pretty girl who looked into the camera with a sad, shy smile. On a yellow Post-It note on the back of the picture, the following lines were written in a precise cursive script: "I think you're my father. If you are, I'd like to visit you this summer. Call me if this is okay. My name is Anne." There was a Los Angeles area phone number written at the bottom of the note.

Robert carefully set the picture down on the wobbly TV tray that doubled for an end table next to his large worn sitting chair. He wiped instinctively at his eyes when his vision began to blur and was mildly surprised to find that he was crying. He sat in the growing dark of the afternoon, and with the shadows came long-suppressed memories of those troubling days. For the first time in years he thought about Kathy and about how badly he'd treated her. He thought about his many other failed relationships over the intervening years that proved out how he was incapable of love and how he was unworthy of decent human company. And he thought about how he'd never once tried to find out if he had a child, much less help support her financially, or in any way participate in her life. He felt shame and panic at the idea of meeting his daughter now. Tears flowed freely down his unshaven face, while occasional sobs broke out from him in sharp isolated barks. Finally, after more than an hour sitting motionless in his big chair, Robert's tortured thoughts began to turn to the dark and heavy Colt revolver waiting patiently, loaded and ready for him in one of the polished teak drawers under the etched glass doors of his gun cabinet.

Johanna Brakley stamped the snow off of her boots while she complained loudly to Box and Lady, her two dogs – a yellow lab and German shepherd respectively – about the difficulty of getting around in the dead of winter, and all of the general infirmities attendant with her advanced years. Both of the dogs were accustomed to her cranky monologues and didn't stir from their places near the warm fire. After the long task of pulling off her outer rubber boots, she grumbled her way into the kitchen. Her general complaints about the weather turned into specific accusations about how often the phone lines go out every winter, and how it didn't much matter, since not one of her three grown children, or her eleven grandchildren bothered to call her more than once in a blue moon anyway. Box – whose name used to be Boxer, because of how he used to punch at his litter-mates with his front paws during play – raised his head when Johanna went into the kitchen, hoping it meant they were about to be fed. He lowered it again after there were no dinner-heralding sounds from the electric can opener.

A few minutes later, Johanna came back out of the kitchen unwinding a length of white half-inch clothesline rope she'd taken from the utility drawer. Both dogs watched curiously as she pulled one of the wooden dining-room chairs under the big open beam running across the center of the room overhead.

"And it would kill them to actually come visit me once in a while?" she said, pulling herself up to stand on the seat of the chair. "Not a one of them's any damned good."

She tied a slip-knot loop in one end of the rope and wound several loops of the other end around the overhead beam, carefully tying it off with a number of basic, solid square-knots. Slipping the makeshift noose over her head, she said, "This will make them wish they treated me better," then she kicked the chair out from under her feet. Both of her dogs whimpered mournfully as she dangled over their heads, the firelight throwing a giant slowly-rocking shadow of her against the far wall.

At the same time Johanna Brakley was fashioning her rope into a noose and Robert Olney cocked the hammer back on the gun placed against his head, Tammy Heller ran her father's straight razor along her wrist in a wet, red series of long, deep, wonderfully satisfying cuts. She was nearly sixteen, but her parents still wouldn't let her wear makeup, get her ears pierced, or go out on car dates. This will show them, she said to herself as she cut. "They'll be sorry when they find me," she said out loud. But her parents would never find her and never be sorry, because less than 15 minutes earlier, on the way back from Video Hut – with rented tapes of Gladiator and Random Hearts – her father, overcome by the pressure of so many mounting bills, had purposely steered their car off of the road. The car rolled down thirty feet of steep embankment, cutting through the snow and gaining speed, until it plunged through the ice covering Little Trail River. Tammy's parents died quickly, belted into their seats side by side, trapped under the freezing waters.

Deputy Town Marshall, Carl Danyow hadn't filed a tax return in seven years, and knew it was only a matter of time before the IRS caught up to him. He sat in his parked patrol car, letting the engine idle as he played with the holster snap of his Patent Leather, Sam Brown pistol belt.

Margaret Novak felt guilty about letting her husband's business partner kiss her last night, when he'd dropped her off after bowling league. She found a carton of Unisom SleepTabs and a bulk sized bottle of Bayer Aspirin in the medicine cabinet. In the high cupboard over the stove she found a half-bottle of whiskey to wash them down with.

Duane Gilbert sat in his garage, letting it fill up with engine fumes from his softly rumbling pickup truck. He'd missed another deadline and was just too damned weary to come up with any more excuses for his editor. A short suicide note was his last piece of writing over a career spanning more than thirty years. He felt vaguely proud of the note's brevity as he slipped into the comforting darkness.

Chapter Two
A Hero of Old

Countless arguments occur over which is first, but there is no question that Pandora, in the State of Coventry, is the second most famous city in the world. On a bright Spring morning, Janet Garrow, having arrived in the city less than an hour earlier, found herself deep in the bad part of town, the Pandora neighborhood called Little Babylon, pounding on a third-floor apartment door of a rundown four-story brownstone.

"Keep your pants on! I'm coming!" she heard, a muffled voice yell from the other side of the thick door – a solid, real-wood relic from back when such things were built to last. After a wait of some minutes she heard the clicks of the deadbolt being thrown back and finally the door opened. Framed in the wide open doorway, backlit by sunlight drifting in through a single, dirty apartment window, Janet recognized the man she'd flown across the nation that morning to see. He was a few inches over six-foot tall and looked to be in his middle to late thirties, though she knew he was considerably older. He had blue eyes, short dark hair and several days' growth of beard. He was also naked except for a pair of boxer shorts, in a blue and yellow tartan pattern, and his well-known – in better days – pilot's cap with its trademark gold wolf's-head badge, pinned above its brim. His body was bulky to the point of being pudgy, but hinted at solid muscle underneath.

"What?" the man barked down at Janet. His eyes were squinty and crusted with recent sleep. "Why are you pounding on my door in the middle of the morning?"

"It's actually almost noon," Janet said.

"My point exactly," the man growled. "Decent people are still in bed at this hour. I'm not interested in what you're selling. I don't want to subscribe to your magazine, sign your petition, take your survey, or change my long-distance service." His breath smelled of stale beer and his body gave off the faint burnt-cork odor of having gone several days without bathing.

"I'm not here to try to sell you anything, sir. In fact I flew here from Philadelphia specifically to see you."

"Why?" he said, after taking a long moment to look her over, from head to toe and back again. She was about five and a half feet tall, maybe a bit taller, and was slim and shapely. She had an attractive face and light brown hair, pinned behind her head in a tight knot, that left just a few lose strands artfully hanging down the back of her neck. She wore an expensive gray business suit; a jacket over a knee-length skirt; the type corporate lawyers wear while closing the deal on billion-dollar mergers.

"You're Beowulf, right?" she said, already knowing the answer. "The famous one from history, the hero of old, monster slayer, and all that?"

"I used to be," he answered. "But that was a long time ago. Now I'm just a tired old man who can tell when someone's about to waste a lot of his time."

"And until twenty years ago you used to be Coventry's most famous Licensed Private Hero," Janet continued, betting that he would be just polite enough not to close the door in her face, if she kept talking. "But you lost your license when…"

"I don't mean to be rude, young lady, but I don't need to have the low-points of my personal history repeated back to me by a stranger in my doorway – no matter how pretty she is."

"I'm sorry, Mister Beowulf, and you're absolutely right. It was rude of me to start in before I've even introduced myself. My name is Janet Garrow, and I'm an agent of the Saint George Group. It's also known as the Valentine Institute, after the name of its founder. No doubt you've heard of it." She stuck her hand out and boldly kept it there when the famous old hero didn't immediately take it.

"No, I haven't," Beowulf said. He reluctantly shook the woman's hand, loathe to insult her by refusing it, but knowing the gesture would only encourage her to continue talking.

"That's surprising," she said. "Granted, we've only been in operation for a few years, but our media coverage has been copious and favorable."

"My loss for not keeping up with current events. I'm certain you're all the rage," he said in a quiet monotone that took most – but not all – of the sting out of his sarcasm.

"If you don't mind, I'd like to take a few minutes to familiarize you with our work."

"And why would that be of any interest to me, Miss Garrow?"

"Because the Institute sent me out here to offer you a job. May I come in?"

"No."

"Then may I take you out to lunch – or breakfast rather – while I explain in more detail what we have in mind?"

"No."

"May I ask why not?"

"Because I'm a throwback to a lost age, when social rules were different. Letting you pay for my lunch would obligate me to give actual consideration to whatever it is you're trying to sell me, and I don't want to do that."

"The Institute's already paid a considerable sum to fly me out here. Another twenty dollars for a meal won't make much difference."

"Maybe not to you, but I didn't invite you out here, so however much money you wasted on your flight is none of my business."

"Forget breakfast then. Will you give me a few minutes to listen to our offer – without any obligation?"

"I'd rather go back to bed."

"Let me try a different tack, Mister Beowulf. It's our understanding that you've supported yourself over the past few years by doing odd jobs and piecework. I'll pay you a hundred dollars cash for an hour of your time this afternoon, after you've caught up on your sleep of course."

"And what would I have to do?"

"Show up at a public place of your choosing and listen to what I have to say, after which you can walk away one hundred dollars richer, free and clear."

"Okay, Miss Garrow, you've worn me down. You can buy an hour of my time today, but I'll need five dollars of that in advance."

"Why?"

"Because the YMCA down the block charges a dollar to use their showers, and it'll take another four bucks to run a load of laundry at the Wash N' Walk. I don't imagine either of us would enjoy it if I met you in public in my current condition."

A few minutes later, and five dollars poorer, Janet was back on the street, looking for her cab. The driver had promised to wait, but didn't.

They met shortly after five that afternoon, at the Four Angry Spirits Chinese Buffet Palace, located just north of

Little Babylon in the more upscale Belladonna neighborhood. Beowulf was much transformed when he arrived. He'd showered and shaved. He wore a clean white cotton dress shirt tucked into a pair of old, but freshly washed, blue denim pants. He'd also added a green silk necktie that was only slightly stained. When he was shown to Janet's table, he paused there only long enough to tip his hat once and drape his brown leather flight jacket over the back of his chair, before heading directly to the buffet tables. He returned minutes later with two large dinner plates piled high with food. At first Janet assumed he'd gotten dinner for both of them, and was mildly upset that he didn't bother to ask what she wanted. But when he placed both plates on his side of the table, she realized he hadn't intended to inflict some remnant of old world gallantry on her.

"You'd better go get yours now, if you plan to eat something before it's all gone," Beowulf said, as he sat across from her. "I'll have their trays cleaned out by my fourth or fifth trip. In all of history, no buffet restaurant's ever made money off of me, and none ever will." His plates were piled high with all manner of chicken, pork and shrimp dishes, cooked in a dozen different spicy sauces that had flowed into one hot, wet melange. Paying her no further attention, he drew his set of chopsticks out of their red paper envelope, with a dramatic flourish, like an ancient knight unsheathing his sword for deadly battle. Then he tucked his head towards the first of his plates and dug in with determination.

Janet visited the buffet line and returned with a single plate which held a more modest serving of chicken and broccoli over fried rice. "What is it with you and that hat?" she said, resuming her seat.

"What do you mean?" he said between bites.

"You mentioned this morning that you were an old ways

sort of fellow, yet you don't remove your hat in a restaurant. And back at your apartment, you were willing to answer the door in your underwear, but had to put your hat on first?"

"That's what you want to pay me a hundred dollars an hour to talk about?" He used his chopsticks with such dexterity that Janet – reluctant to risk looking clumsy in front of her guest – contented herself with a normal western fork.

"No, but it seemed unusual enough to get my attention," she said.

"We can talk about the oddities of my sartorial habits if you want," he said. "For what you're paying, we can talk about whatever you like. But at the end of the hour, I'm out that door."

"What happened to your obligation to fairly consider my proposal, since I'm buying the dinner?"

"That's why you're only buying your own dinner. As soon as you pay me the rest of my fee, I plan to pay for my half of the meal, so there's no obligation on my part to do anything more than listen while you talk. I can listen just fine while eating, so maybe you should get started on your speech, before time runs out." Beowulf drained his tall glass of iced tea in one long gulp and then looked around for the tiny Chinese girl that was wandering around the dining area with two huge pitchers of tea and ice-water.

"Very well, Mister Beowulf, I'll get right to the point. And since the clock is ticking down so resolutely, I hope you'll pardon my candor. At the Institute, we're aware of the unfortunate circumstances under which you lost your hero's license, and the years of civil court actions that followed, which drained both your fortune and reputation. Since then – between frequent bouts of drunkenness – you've done day-labor work and odd jobs to scrape together enough money each year to file a petition to get your license restored. But every year the St. Clair family uses their considerable fortune and political muscle to get your petition quashed."

"Who can blame them?" Beowulf said, still trying to get the eye of the iced-tea girl. "I got their precious little girl killed."

"So they claim, but we think you got a raw deal."

"And you're here to put all that to right?" Finally getting the serving girl's attention, he waved his empty glass in the universal "I need a refill" gesture.

"Not a chance," she said. "Victor St. Clair wields too much power in this town. As long as he lives, you'll never get another hero's license in this state."

"You're probably right," Beowulf said, "but one of the advantages of immortality is that I'm almost guaranteed to outlive the bastard. I'll get back in action some day. I can afford to wait."

"I imagine so, but you don't have to. The Institute has influence in Pennsylvania in the same way that Old Man St. Clair has in Coventry. We can have you vetted and licensed within twenty-four hours of the moment you come to work for us."

"Doing what?"

"Hunting and killing monsters of course. That was always your forte, and it's what the Institute is all about."

"Okay, Miss Garrow, you've captured my attention. Let me hit the buffet tables for a refill and you can tell me all about your Institute. We can start with things like salary and benefits."

They ended up talking for many hours, long into the evening, much to the consternation of the restaurant staff, once it became clear to them that the big man in the pilot's cap intended to keep eating until all of the food was gone.

Chapter Three
The Monster Maker

Beowulf had almost nothing in the way of personal af-
fairs to settle before moving across the country, so he was
able to join Janet Garrow on the red-eye flight out of Pandora
that same evening. A single half-full Army surplus duffel
bag was enough to contain the sum total of his worldly pos-
sessions at that time in his life. Janet installed him in the per-
manent suite the Institute kept at the Ritz Carlton Hotel for
visiting VIP's, which would be his to use until he found an
apartment of his own. By the next morning he was at his new
job.

The Saint George Group's offices took up all of the 55th
and 56th floors of One Liberty Place, a giant steel and glass
structure that dominated Philadelphia's Center City skyline.
Janet met him in the spacious lobby and took him immediately in hand.

"Normally on your first day you'd have a fairly light
schedule," she said. She was dressed again in another "power
lawyer" ensemble, and showed none of the effects of having
gotten a mere four hours sleep the night before. "I'd shop
you around to the department heads to get all of the paperwork done for licensing, insurance, medical coverage and the
like. But there's some big business afoot this morning, which
means we're going to fast-track your in-processing, starting
with a visit to see the director."

She hooked an arm through one of his and quick-marched
him down a wide, burgundy-carpeted hallway. They passed
a series of regularly spaced doors labeled with unfamiliar

terms like, Lycanthropology and Vampiretics. Others were marked using more ordinary words that nevertheless combined in ways that hinted at occult purposes. He wondered what could go on in an office called Weird Distribution Statistics. The hall ended in a massive set of carved doors that looked as if they'd been transplanted from the temple of some lost civilization. These doors weren't labeled in any way, but Beowulf didn't need another brass plaque to know that this would be the boss' digs. Janet knocked once and entered without waiting for a reply.

"Beowulf, hero of old," she said, "meet our director, Doctor Pindahl Valentine, otherwise known as The Monster Maker."

"Mister Beowulf, I am delighted to finally meet you," Doctor Valentine said. He stood up from behind his desk – on unsteady legs and only with the help of a stout cane – and leaned over it, offering his hand to the famous hero. Valentine was tall, slim and dark-skinned. His blacker than night hair was cut short and had a slight dusting of gray over each temple. He looked to be East Indian, but spoke with an accent forged in the venerable halls of Eton. He wore a navy blue, double-breasted, pinstriped suit that hung on his body like a tailor's dearest fantasy.

"Normally," he continued, "I'd insist on passing a leisurely few hours grilling you all about your many past adventures. But things are a bit hectic this morning and I'm afraid our first meeting will have to be a short one. Too bad. I was dying to find out how you managed to survive the dragon. Don't you know you're supposed to be dead?"

"It's a long story," Beowulf said, "but the short version is: journalists back then weren't any more accurate than they are today. They don't often let facts get in the way of a good story."

Valentine invited Beowulf to sit in one of the two red leather-padded armchairs in front of the large desk. Unlike the outside office area, which was sleek and modern in design, the director's chambers were done in an old-world style of oiled leathers and polished woods. Except for the large window behind the desk – which looked out over Philadelphia's Olde City and Delaware Riverfront area – and a couple of smaller doors which led to places unseen, all of the available surface areas were taken up with floor to ceiling bookshelves, packed with many an ancient volume.

Sometime following the introductions, Janet Garrow had quietly slipped out of the office, closing the doors behind her, leaving the two men alone together. After seeing his guest seated, Valentine carefully lowered himself into his own large chair, leaning his cane on his side of the desk, once it was no longer needed.

"We need to move along quickly this morning," he said, "so I'll inflict on you only the most truncated version of my usual welcoming speech. The purpose of this institute is fairly simple: to identify and destroy the monsters which plague our world. You won't find us to be a very politically correct organization. We don't want to help these dangerous creatures reform, or waste time discovering the root causes of their depredations on the world's civilized communities. In fact we aren't much interested in understanding them at all, except to the extent that such understanding helps us hunt and destroy them."

"That kind of attitude isn't very popular in today's world," Beowulf said. "I'm surprised I didn't trip over an army of Supernaturals-rights protesters camped out on your doorstep."

"We're a relatively new organization and so far we've benefited from not being well known. But, assuming we do our work properly, the protests and lawsuits will come. That's why the first thing I did in creating this institute is assemble a first rate legal team composed of the most vicious predatorial bastards in international law. They call themselves the Wrecking Crew, and for Christmas presents last year they produced T-shirts with the picture of a blood-drenched pit-bull holding a severed human arm in its teeth. I love those guys. If anyone can keep us free to do our work, they can."

"That begs the question, what do you consider monsters?"

"That is the essential question, isn't it?" Valentine said. "Monsters, by the Institute's definition – which really means by my definition – are any creature that can't behave; that preys upon civilization. Such things are only judged individually, on a case by case basis, and not by any of the obvious groups that have suffered under the label of 'monster' in the past. I'm not interested in wiping out lycanthropy or vampirism, or any other broad subset of the so-called Supernature. In fact, vampires for example, through their strictly enforced dietary laws, are surprisingly good at keeping their own house in order.

"At the Institute we search out those creatures, both mundane and supernatural, who have proven themselves to be irredeemable predators on society. With our limited resources, we can't possibly find and destroy them all, so we try to single out the very worst of them, and once we do, I write them on my master list. At that moment, in my definition, they have officially become monsters. In a sense, the very act of adding them to the master list has officially made them a monster, which is why some unidentified wit on the staff saddled me with the nickname Monster Maker. The name caught on, and I seem to be stuck with it."

"How big is the list?" Beowulf said.

"It started out as a ten-most-wanted list and quickly grew into a hundred-most-wanted. I'm trying to hold it at that number, but it isn't easy."

"And my job is to hunt them down and kill them, thereby freeing up spaces on your list for you to add others?"

"Essentially, yes, Mister Beowulf. You've defined the heart of your duties. But it's not your job alone. You are the third private hero we've recruited. I believe you're acquainted with Prester John?"

"Yeah. We ran into each other once or twice during the Great War. He's a good man."

"And we've also got William Churchill on the payroll," Valentine said. "He used to practice under the registered trade name of the Blackheart Kid."

"Isn't he the gunslinger? The guy with those ghost-guns? I read he claims they're the spirits of Jimmy Hickok's pistols. What's he calling himself now?"

"He hasn't chosen a new trade name, but once he passed his thirtieth birthday, he decided any name with 'Kid' as a part of it was something less than poetic. His skill with those deadly weapons of his has only improved though, so he could call himself Bambi and I'd still be happy to have him. I assume you'll want to resume using Beowulf as your registered trade name?"

"Yeah. I've never been one for made-up names. So who decides which monsters I go after? Do I pick them off of your list, or do you assign our missions?"

"A little of both, I imagine," Valentine said. "We're still working out the specific protocols. But your first assignment has already been determined. You and Miss Garrow are on your way to Montana first thing in the morning, which is why we need to rush you through in-processing today. Normally I wouldn't throw you into the thick of things so quickly, but both of the others are out on other missions, and our Miss Garrow, though an able investigator, isn't a fighter. I don't want to send her into possible harms way without someone to look after her."

"What's the assignment?"

"Sometime last month, the entire population of a remote Montana town committed suicide. I'd like you to find out why."

Chapter Four
Diversions

Freelance pilot Eddie Kilmer entered the large office he privately called The Shadows, due as much to the sense of oppression he always felt on entering the place, as to the subdued lighting. As usual the dark man – always a backlit silhouette – was in his place behind the big desk, and the tall, inhuman creature that served and guarded him stood immobile and silent against one wall.

"Mister Kilmer, I'm pleased you were able to come see us again on short notice," the dark man said.

"No problem," Kilmer said. "If you've got more work you need done, Kilmer Air Service is at your service." From past experience he knew the guardian creature had silently shifted its position to stand behind him, as soon as he entered the office. To say that it made him nervous would be an understatement. The thing stood at least seven feet tall and seemed to be made out of living blood red stone. That thing was why reasonable men were afraid of the dark.

"No, Mister Kilmer, I have no further use for you, but I wanted to personally thank you for the quality of your work for me last month. It's so rare to find such a high level of professionalism in our modern world, that I've decided to add a large bonus to your final payment."

"You've already been more than generous," Kilmer said, brightening considerably. "But I'm not about to turn down more money. Pa Kilmer didn't raise no fools. I guess you got all the data you needed for your experiment then? The tests turned out okay?"

"Most definitely, Mister Kilmer, the testing turned out perfectly, so well in fact that I've been able to move up our schedule, to the final stage of the experiment, by a full week. We've now entered the official 'covering our tracks' phase."

"I don't get what you mean by that," Kilmer said.

But then Kilmer felt a heavy, clawed hand come down hard on his shoulder and knew in that instant what the dark man meant. There was a mercifully brief crunching of bones and then silence again in The Shadows.

•

The next day Beowulf and Janet Garrow boarded a public flight from Philadelphia to Dillon, Montana, with one stop in Chicago for a change in planes. The night before, Beowulf had sent his one suit out to be cleaned and pressed. Taking a cue from the refined dress habits of Miss Garrow, Doctor Valentine, and each one of the Institute's various department heads he'd met the day before, the normally rumpled hero decided to make an effort to blend in a bit better with the pack. He'd showed up at the airport in his suit, a clean white shirt, and newly dry-cleaned green tie. His ever-present pilot's cap was the single off note in his generally businesslike appearance. It was inevitable then that Janet showed up dressed for the snowy and rugged outdoors of the high-elevation areas of Montana. She wore khakis that had seen plenty of use, a blue quilted vest, and big, snow-stomper boots. Along with her single bag she carried a heavy parka-like jacket that was covered in an uncountable number of snap-pockets and zipper pouches.

"You show up to the office dressed like a bum," Janet said when she saw him, "but you dress in your best suit to go into the field? You're an odd man, Beowulf."

"I have outdoors clothes in my bag," Beowulf said, with quiet dignity. Only the barest touch of embarrassment colored his cheeks.

Once seated on the plane, in the first class section of course, Janet immediately began to brief her partner from her copy of the mission's case file.

"Diversion, Montana," she said. "Population 78, give or take. History: It was originally called Clark's Diversion, because the place was first discovered by the explorer William Clark, who'd split off from the main Lewis and Clark expedition for a few days. In his journal he mentioned the area as having a wonderful cutthroat trout stream, where they camped for one night. That seems to be why Abner Little homesteaded the place almost 50 years later. It's a tiny town located 18 miles west of Grant, on County Route 324, which climbs up the Rockies to Lemhi Pass, which is where the Lewis and Clark expedition crossed the mountains on the old Lolo Trail. It's a popular hunting and fishing resort in the summer months, but usually entirely snowed-in during the winter."

"Was it snowed-in when everyone killed themselves?" Beowulf asked. He sipped complimentary bourbon over ice, from a real glass.

"Yes it was," she answered, after flipping forward a few pages in the report. "The only access road had been closed off for eight days when it... when they... when the incidents occurred. There's helicopter service out of Dillon, for emergencies, during those times, but no calls were ever made in that time period. That isn't unusual. For the most part the citizens of Diversion are used to hunkering down and waiting out the big snows. They weren't discovered until eleven days ago, when the road was finally cleared from Grant, up to the town."

"Were they all part of the same church?" he asked.

"No. We already thought of that and checked. And unlike mass suicides normally associated with religious cults, they each killed themselves in separate ways. Some ate their guns, some took pills, and some jumped from high places, of which I suspect the area is supplied in abundance. Some left notes and some didn't. Except for the timing, and the fact that all of them opted to do it, there seems to be no common elements to the suicides."

Janet continued, reading the report in its entirety, but there was nothing more to be gleaned from the information they had. They'd have to wait until arriving in Dillon for more facts on which to speculate. When they ran out of business matters to discuss, the conversation naturally turned towards personal matters.

"I was quite a fan of yours when I was a kid," Janet said, while they were flying over the lower tip of Lake Eerie. "I made dad subscribe to the Sunday edition of the Pandora Times, which had that magazine insert that covered the adventures of all of Coventry's famous private heroes. Dad was stationed in Germany at the time, so we'd get it a week or more late, but I didn't care. The Stars and Stripes bookstore on the post carried your comic books, so I collected those too."

"They were horrible," Beowulf said, crunching the ice from his third drink. "In the six years they were published, they didn't cover one single case as it really happened."

"Who cares? I mostly wanted them for the painted covers. They always showed you with your shirt ripped and your muscles showing through."

"Which you can see was a damned lie," Beowulf said, patting the paunch of his considerable belly.

"Okay but that was twenty years ago. Everyone puts on weight as they age."

"I don't age, Miss Garrow. I'm immortal, remember? The sad truth is I was always a pudgy bastard, today, twenty years ago, and centuries ago."

"Well, I liked them anyway. I liked those puffy pants you wore too. What are they called? The kind of pants safari guys used to wear in old black and white films."

"They were called Jodhpurs, and I never wore a pair of those prissy things in my life."

"You're poking holes in all my fondest memories," Janet said with an affected pout. "I had a schoolgirl crush on you because of those paintings."

"It was James Bama you had a crush on," Beowulf said. "He's the artist who painted those covers. Except for a vague resemblance to my face, and my trademark cap, he made everything else up."

"So how did you get to be an immortal?" Janet asked, after an uncomfortable lull in the conversation that Beowulf made no effort to fill.

"The same dragon that killed me, made me immortal," he answered. "You read the legend, no doubt. I killed the dragon that was preying on my kingdom, but not before it had zapped me several times with its lethal poison. The poison killed me; that part at least the writers got right. But by that time I was covered in the serpent's blood. As you know – or should know, if you're going to be in this business – bathing in dragon's blood is one of the few ways for us lowly humans to gain immortality and various other great and magical powers."

"So what happened?" Janet said. For a brief moment, she was the eleven-year-old fan girl reborn.

"I became an immortal dead guy. Basically, the poison put me into a long, death-like coma. My young sidekick in that battle, not knowing any better, assumed I was truly dead, and promptly gave me a Viking funeral, with all the bells and whistles customary to one of my rank."

"He burned you?"

"Yup. He put me in a boat, pushed it out into the ocean, and set the damned thing on fire. And by that time the dragon's blood had restored me enough that, though I still couldn't move, I was conscious."

"While you were burning?"

"I was awake and aware during the whole thing; while I burned, while my burned body sank under the sea, and off and on at the bottom of the sea, for the hundred-plus years it took the dragon's blood to rebuild my body, pretty much from scratch."

"Oh my. That must have been horrible."

"Mostly it was boring. Fish and other critters kept eating at me, at the same time the dragon's blood kept trying to rebuild me. For a long time it was a near thing which side would finally win out. But one day I was whole enough to claw my way out of the built up muck and coral infestation, and swim to the surface."

"That's incredible! I'm surprised the experience didn't drive you insane."

"Are you serious? Of course it drove me insane. I was nutty as a bishop for something in the neighborhood of the next two hundred years. But I guess even that was something the dragon's blood insisted on fixing, because one day I began to remember who I was, and the rest – as they say – is history."

"Wow," Janet said, quietly. And then, after a while, "You know, I was going to do my social part and tell you a little about my life so far, but I have nothing to compare with your stories."

"Then I'm going to take a nap," Beowulf said. "Wake me when it's time to change planes."

Chapter Five
The Jimmy Olsen Syndrome

The 63 corpses from Diversion – some had yet to be found, or were in places difficult to get to – had been transported to a large, unheated aircraft hanger in Dillon, where they underwent intense examination from experts in many fields. The FBI was there in force, with agents from their Behavioral Sciences and Forensic Sorcery departments. Various Montana law enforcement officers were there, from state and county levels, and an armed company of the Montana National Guard secured the area surrounding the hanger.

A mention of Doctor Valentine's name was enough to get Janet and Beowulf past the first line of guards, into "officer's territory," which in this case was a green canvas tent, pitched outside of the hanger.

"Someone will be along shortly to escort you in," a helpful lieutenant said for the third time in as many minutes – he was unable to think of any other excuse to talk to the pretty female investigator from Philadelphia. He was dressed in starched and pressed, camouflage Army fatigues. He struck Janet as the type who'd check himself in the mirror frequently, to make sure he was strack, a term of military arcana with no exact civilian equivalent, but which contained elements of "looking good" and "professional" and "squared away." In her childhood, Janet spent many hours polishing her father's boots and brass, to make sure he'd be properly strack, each and every day. Janet despised the young lieutenant on sight. Eventually a polite and eager kid – he couldn't be more than nineteen or twenty – in a dark blue windbreaker, with AWS written across its back in bold yellow letters, arrived to rescue her.

"Janet Garrow and Mister Beowulf?" the kid in the windbreaker said. "I'm Jeff Dobler, with the Federal Bureau of Alchemy, Witchcraft and Sorcery. I've been assigned as your liaison today."

"What horrible things did you do to get stuck babysitting us?" Beowulf said. He'd added a heavy jacket over his suit since they landed. Three days into spring in Montana was a lot like the dead of winter in most other places.

"Once I heard you'd be coming in, I volunteered for the assignment," Dobler said, with a kind of dopey enthusiasm. "It's a step up for me. So far they've had me strictly on gofer duty; getting coffee and fast food, and running every other kind of errand they could think of. Besides, I've been a fan of yours since forever, Mister Beowulf. It's a privilege to show you and Miss Garrow around." He escorted Janet and Beowulf out of the Army command tent and towards the open hanger doors.

"You don't look old enough to have been a fan of mine," Beowulf said. "Unless you were perverse enough to have jumped on the bandwagon long after everyone else had jumped off. I haven't had a public career in more than two decades."

"Oh, I'm older than I look," Dobler said, a slight tinge of petulance coloring his voice. "That's why I always get stuck with the bum assignments. I'm a certified lab technician for the AWS, but everyone calls me "Kid" and won't trust me with anything more vital than making sure they get the right amount of cream and sugar in their coffee. One wit in there even calls me Jimmy Olsen, and laughs like a goon each time he says it."

"Well, we won't make the same mistake, Mister Dobler,"

Janet said, although she'd already started thinking of him as "the kid" in her mind.

"For the record," Dobler continued, addressing Beowulf, "I think you got a raw deal in Coventry. They should never have taken your hero's license away, just because of the St. Clair incident. If you ask me, the quality of private heroes in Pandora has gone down considerably since then. Claudia Nevermore? She's got all the style of a certified public accountant. I can't believe she's the most popular private hero out there, these days. They don't want bold adventurers anymore, they want someone who always has the paperwork filled out and filed correctly. It's all politics, Mister Beowulf. No one knows that better than me."

"Yeah, politics," Beowulf grumbled, his tone of voice a warning that the kid should drop the subject. A cold, drizzling rain had begun to seep down from the iron-gray clouds overhead.

"In any case, I'm pleased to see you back in action again," Dobler said. "Anything you want, anything at all, you just ask me."

"We'll keep that in mind," Janet said. She was a little put off at Dobler's giddy devotion to the old hero, and wondered how she could make it clear to the kid, without seeming petty, that Beowulf, for all of his fame, was the junior partner on this case. She'd already begun to miss the attention from the preening Army lieutenant.

By then they'd reached the entrance to the hanger. After showing their various identifications – yet again – to the guard stationed immediately outside, Dobler ushered them in to the mysteries within.

Each body was laid out on its own table. Some were still twisted in the odd positions in which they were found, frozen solid after long exposure to the bitter cold of more than three week's exposure to winter in the high foothills of the Rocky Mountains. Men and women in white coats and surgical gloves hovered about the corpses, darting from one table to another, like bumblebees gathering nectar from a field of flowers. They clipped and cut, stabbed and swabbed, taking redundant samples from each cadaver, for an endless number of separate laboratory tests.

In another part of the hanger, other scientists and their assistants sorted through a host of bagged and tagged artifacts that had also been transplanted from the death-town called Diversion. They were the suicide weapons, recovered at the scene. They were knives, guns, razors, pill bottles, ropes and all the other implementia of single-serving destruction. There were two complete gas ranges that had been flown down from Diversion, suspended under the belly of Army helicopters. In the back of the hanger there were five full automobiles – three sedans and two pickup trucks – that had been the instruments of death for a total of seven of the victims. One of the cars had been chopped out of the frozen waters of the Little Trail River. There were even a number of blood-spattered rocks there, from those victims who ended their lives by throwing themselves off of some high place. Each item would be examined and reexamined, tested and retested. Over the coming months, each separate object would generate reams of paperwork and megabytes of computer data.

Other people milled about in the giant room, brightly lit by the hundreds of portable lamps jerryrigged throughout the overhead structures. Some were in military uniform, others were outfitted in various police uniforms, while others still were in civilian clothes, but wore blue windbreakers, over their jackets, that identified them as agents of the FBI, or the AWS, or one of a dozen other federal agencies. The constant hum of a hundred continuous conversations filled the vast enclosed space.

"These are the operatives from the Saint George Group," Dobler said, introducing Janet and Beowulf to a tall man who wore a weather-scarred face, under the short bristles of a silver and black crew-cut.

"Glad to have you aboard," the man said, taking notice of the sudden spike of resentment that flitted across Janet's face when he chose to shake hands with Beowulf before offering his hand to her. "I'm Doctor Gil Franklin, from the Center for Disease Control. I'm but one of the too many chiefs and not enough Indians who're supposed to be running this great mess of an investigation. Your director, Valentine, stole my best forensic sorcerer last year."

"I guess that would be Doctor Kacirk?" Janet said.

"The very one," Franklin said. "My revenge will come the first time Valentine is foolhardy enough to sit down to a friendly game of poker with the woman. I'd like to bring her in on this. We've gotten some odd trace substances, in most of the tissue samples we've taken so far, that none of our men or machines has been able to identify."

"If you like, I'll fax the readouts to her immediately," Janet said. "And then we can overnight some hair clippings, blood and saliva swabs…"

"We'll have to wait on sending out any actual tissue samples," Franklin interrupted. "We haven't even worked out a preliminary vector theory on this X-bug yet. Until we do, nothing leaves this building."

"You've determined it's some sort of biological agent?" Janet said.

"No."

"But you referred to it as a bug," she said.

"Right," Franklin said. "Sloppy methodology on our part, but we had to call it something. At first we called it Agent-X, but that was too distracting. It was a name more appropriate to a comic book character, so we changed it to keep the silly conversations to a minimum."

"But your current theory is that this is the result of some outside force which acted on the townspeople?" Janet said.

"Yeah," Franklin said. "We've already discounted that it was some planned event by all of the victims. The context of some of their suicide notes imply that each of them acted on their own, not aware that everyone else in town suddenly had the same notion to end it all. Many notes were addressed to friends and family members who also killed themselves. If it was an organized mass-suicide, they would have known those people wouldn't be around to find their notes. In lieu of conflicting evidence, our investigations are directed at a chemical, biological or magical agent that induced mass suicide. Bug-X, for now."

"And is your Bug-X a natural thing, or did someone bring it to town?" Beowulf said.

"That's the 64 thousand dollar question, isn't it?" Franklin said. "We don't know. So far the crime scene hasn't produced any evidence one way or the other."

"But you're treating the town as a crime scene?" Janet said.

"Wouldn't you?"

"Point taken."

"We've got another team choppering up to Diversion in a few minutes," Franklin said, "to join those looking for the remaining missing townspeople. We'd love to find at least one of them alive. I can arrange room for you on the bird, if you want to go up there."

"No thanks," Janet said. "The bodies and all of your test results to date are down here. This is where we'll find out what caused this tragedy, so this is where I need to be, for the time being."

"I'd like to go up," Beowulf said.

"That's not possible," Janet said. "We're needed down here."

"I agree that you are," Beowulf said, "but I'm not the investigator half of our team. I won't learn a thing reading lab reports and sniffing around down here, that you or all of these other scientist types won't discover first."

"That's not the point," Janet said. "You're supposed to stay with me."

"Sure, to watch your back," Beowulf said. "But you're surrounded by a couple of hundred heavily-armed soldiers here. I think you're safe enough for a few hours."

"What good would you do up there?" Janet said. "You said yourself, you're no investigator."

"No, but I've lived half my life in the wild places," Beowulf said. "In that time I've learned a thing or two about finding people lost in the woods. I'd like to lend a hand, if I can."

"We could sure use a man like him up there," Dobler offered, earning him a wicked look from Janet, and a perplexed look from Franklin, who was among those who assumed Dobler was merely the kid that brought coffee.

"Fine," Janet finally said, in a voice that made it clear that things were anything but fine. "Do what you want."

Beowulf took her at her word.

•

Minutes later, the dark man finished dictating a series of hurried orders and then slammed the phone down in its cradle, a hot rage burning through him. That execrable adventurer Beowulf had not only come out of retirement, but also had the audacity to stick his meddling nose in the dark man's business. He struggled to calm himself, lest someone notice

the temporary loss of his usual iron control. Slowly, cold determination damped and then replaced his rage. This time the
dark man wouldn't content himself with merely destroying
the hero's career – as when he engineered the St. Clair matter. This time he'd take Beowulf's life.

Chapter Six
Blood From a Stone

The Sikorsky "Black Hawk" UH-60Q medical transport and evacuation helicopter kicked up surprisingly little snow as it settled onto the hard ground, on the eastern edge of Diversion. Most of the snow still remaining at that altitude had been partially melted by the spring sun, and then frozen again during the still-cold nights, so often that it had been transformed from its original powdery state into a solid blanket of opaque, icy hardness. Beowulf slid the side door open as soon as the craft had settled, stepping out onto the hard whiteness. He wore a borrowed green Army parka over warm wool pants and heavy boots. He'd been able to change, finally, into clothing more appropriate to the area, in the pilots' ready room, minutes before lift off.

"I'll join the search and rescue teams in a few minutes," he called back to Sergeant Brown, still in the helicopter's large passenger bay with his eight-man team, "but I want to poke around the town a bit first."

Diversion was stacked in several levels, clinging to the side of the pine-forested hills marching steadily upwards to form the mountains that loomed over the tiny river valley. Only about a dozen buildings made up the downtown area, three of which were the luxurious hunting-lodge hotels that catered to both the merely rich and the extremely rich, who provided most of the town's annual income in one three-month spasm each year. One of the hotels, a four-tiered thing called The Bighorn, was actually built hanging over the steep ledge sloping down to the Little Trail river, so that guests could fish directly from their balconies, without ever leaving the sybaritic comfort of their rooms. There was a general store that was also a sportsman's outfitter; a combination bookstore and video store; a diner called Eat Here or Starve; and a tavern called Kenny's. They lined the short main street across from the three sprawling hotels.

Beowulf took much longer than his promised "few minutes" going through each building. He found the occasional dried bloodspatter trace of where one of the townspeople had done themselves in, but nothing that could help him determine why they had all killed themselves. He moved on.

On the first switchback above the main street, he found a number of residences, and a small medical clinic. Next to the clinic was a cinderblock building that boasted at being the Diversion Town Masonic Temple, number 18033, which was next door to a white multi-denominational church, with a real, steepled bell tower. Finally, just before the next switchback, and after a tall stand of lodgepole pines, Beowulf came to the town's only gas station, which also housed the Post Office, town hall, and police station, among its attached cluster of small offices. In the one-room police station he found everything he needed to solve most of the mystery. He left the police station thirty minutes after first entering it, and went off in search of the rescue crews, to help find the remaining bodies.

The monster rose up from behind a snow-crowned boulder after Beowulf had passed close by its hiding place. Beowulf was following the foot-trail of one of the search and rescue crews, up the hill, into the woods, when the thing attacked him. Had the monster made any of the tiny nervous movements that any living creature makes, even while holding still, the veteran hero of a thousand battles would have detected it. Had the monster even breathed, Beowulf would have heard it. But the thing neither breathed nor moved, holding perfectly, lifelessly still, until the moment came to strike. It took Beowulf entirely by surprise. He caught barely a glimpse of red stony flesh under a large gray parka, before its massive fists fell on his head and body.

The monster's first blow ripped open the tough skin of Beowulf's face, spraying wet red onto the snow. The second caught him low on his side, under one arm, and tossed his body high up and yards away in a comic arc of ragdoll antics – a flailing, tumbling satire of flight. Beowulf landed hard, but came up instantly, ready – finally – for deadly battle. He intended to charge his enemy, but found the creature already closing on him with blurring speed.

It was at least seven feet tall and the color of rust or dried blood. It was shaped like a rough sketch of a man, a statue that had been abandoned early by its sculptor, after only the basic approximations of human features had been chipped out in bold, simple detail. Its chest was a massive structure, containing whatever screaming sorcerous engine that fed unlimited power to its oversized arms.

In the ancient days of his youth, long before he'd done battle with the dragon, Beowulf had the strength of thirty grown men in the grip of each hand. He could swim seven days and seven nights in the northern seas in winter, wearing a full suit of armor. His power was great enough to rend Grendel limb from limb, in unarmed battle. Since being washed in the blood of the dragon, his strength had only increased. When the monster closed with him, Beowulf pummeled it with fists that could shatter boulders. Dozens of blows were landed on the creature, which made no attempts to avoid them. Each deadly strike filled the tiny valley with sounds like great explosions. None of it had any effect.

Then Beowulf tried to pin the creature's arms and wrestle

it off of the ground. It seemed heavier than solid stone, as if it were forged of the magic adamants that only the immortal troll smiths of the Under Earth could work. It smiled down at Beowulf and then broke his grip with an exaggerated shrug of its arms. It laid its terrible hands on the hero and began to strip off flesh and grind bone.

"You should have stayed in retirement," the monster said, as it worked one gore-slicked fist into his belly and up under his rib cage.

Its eyes were two small pebbles of obsidian. Fearsome heat radiated from the monster, melting a pool of steaming water from the snow around them. Beowulf remained conscious for a surprisingly long time. He faded to the sound of popping and crackling fireworks. A celebration perhaps, to welcome him into the underworld?

Chapter Seven
Chain of Command

After an immeasurable time floating in absolute dark, itinerant pinpoints of light began to pierce the veil, little firefly things that flared briefly then died again. These increased in number and frequency, gradually, until their combined gravity was such that they began to collide and fall together, like great stars and planets that form from the tumbling dust of space. Finally, the gathering fragments of light and color reached their critical mass and ignited into a misty impression of Janet Garrow's face, hanging over him, filling his tired and retracted field of vision. The liquid face flowed and rippled, and from some unimaginable distance came the words, "Welcome back to the land of the living, partner."

"Where?" he tried to say, though numbness and pain, two warrior deities, locked in mortal combat, conspiring to prevent him.

"You're in the hospital, in Dillon, and probably shouldn't try to speak yet," the kind voice said, while the image hovering over him continued to resolve, becoming ever more Janet-like with each passing moment. "You were medivaced here, after Sergeant Brown's team found you. He said you were in pretty bad shape. They assumed you were dead at first." The voice, which seemed curiously connected to the image of Janet, receded again, and sometime afterwards blackness returned to overwhelm him.

Beowulf was more lucid when he woke again. Janet wasn't in the room, but Jeff Dobler, the eager-faced AWS lab tech, was there. "Wow, I can't believe you're still alive," he said.

"That Army sergeant told us you were all ripped open when they found you, with your intestines and everything spread all over the snow. He said you were delirious and trying to stuff them back in when they got to you."

"If my guts were still on the outside when the wound closed up, they'd have gotten cut off and I would have been unconscious a lot longer while they grew back," Beowulf said, in a strained whisper. "I'd have been down for weeks at least. I couldn't afford to be out of action that long."

"You won't be back in action for a while, anyway," Dobler said. "The doctors say you'll have to stay in the hospital at least a month."

"Nonsense," Beowulf said. "I'll be out of here tonight, if you give me a hand, kid."

"Are you going to start with that too?" Dobler said. His head dropped, as if he was suddenly intensely interested in something on the polished tile floor. Beowulf realized he was a fan who'd just been insulted by his hero.

"Sorry," Beowulf said. "I didn't mean to insult you, or even single you out. Considering how long I've been alive, everyone qualifies as a kid to me."

"Oh, that's okay. I guess I can understand that," Dobler said, shyly reestablishing eye contact. "What is it you wanted me to do, to help you get better?"

"I can repair the rest of my injuries in an hour or so, but I need fuel to power the job. I need you to bring me food, lots of food, as much as you can find. Think of the most you could possibly imagine ten men eating, then double it."

"I don't know," Dobler said. "I promised Miss Garrow that I'd stay with you while she got a shower and a few hours sleep."

"To what purpose?" Beowulf said.

"What do you mean? To look after you, I guess."

"Then keep your promise to her and look after me by getting me something to eat. Right now, the more I eat, the faster I heal. No doctor or bed rest is going to do more for me."

After her shower and nap, Janet Garrow returned to Beowulf's hospital room, only to find a scene of horror. The room was awash in trash. The floor was covered in bags and Styrofoam cartons and paper wrappers from a dozen fast food restaurants. A hundred twisted foil single-serving condiment packs stained the formerly clean tile floor with ketchup, mustard and mayonnaise. Beowulf had a couple of large grocery store paper bags on the bed with him. In one hand he was holding most of a head of lettuce over one of the bags. He held a jumbo-sized bottle of blue cheese dressing in the other hand. He poured dressing over the head of lettuce and shoved his food-stained face down to eat it, while it dripped a steady flow of white, chunky ooze into the bag. He came up for air only long enough to set the bottle of salad dressing down and pick up a greasy fried chicken drumstick. While he ate that, Dobler set another four full bags of McDonald's hamburgers on his bed, balancing them on the shifting blankets wherever he could find room. Janet was too shocked to do anything but stand silently in the doorway.

"So Sergeant Brown and his men saw most of the fight with the big red creature," Dobler said, obviously continuing a conversation that had begun long before she arrived. "They were able to drive it off with small arms fire, which is damned lucky for you, because they said it was beginning the process of ripping you into separate pieces when they showed up."

"That's weird," Beowulf said, his voice distorted by a mouth full of fish sandwich, "that gunfire would frighten it off, because rifle fire doesn't do much harm to me, and this critter was boat-loads tougher than I ever was on my best day. But far be it from me to question providence." He was sitting up in bed and had removed all of the tubes and wires that had been attached to him when Janet had last been there.

"What the hell are you doing?" Janet finally interrupted. She stepped gingerly into the room, carefully avoiding contact with any one of a hundred crumpled pieces of filth covering the floor. In addition to her purse, carried on a strap under one arm, she carried a tight roll of clothing under the other.

"Lunch," was all that Beowulf said, before stuffing another sandwich into his mouth.

"This is an amazing thing to see, Miss Garrow," Dobler said, with undisguised enthusiasm. "An hour ago he was so weak he could barely move. But since then he's been to the bathroom twice, all on his own. His wounds have all healed, forming scars that look like they're a year or more old. Just watching one guy eat so much is incredible, all by itself."

Janet's stomach felt light and trembly with involuntary movement. The beginning dizziness of nausea made her feel unsteady on her feet. The air in the small room was thick with the smell of half a dozen different types of animal grease. And the other smell, coming from the half-open door to the bathroom was too horrible to contemplate.

"Catch her if she faints, Dobler," Beowulf said. He grabbed such a great handful of golden colored fries, out of one of the McDonald's bags, that his fist looked like a giant, glistening daisy blossom.

It took three separate trips for Dobler to get Beowulf's room clean – one to buy a box of large plastic garbage bags, and two more to haul the filled bags out to the hospital's dumpsters. Janet Garrow was coldly furious with the flustered young man, as he bagged the trash and scrubbed the room, cringing under her silent but imperious supervision.

But during those times when Dobler was out of the room, Janet's mood lightened considerably.

"He has a crush on me," Janet told Beowulf, during Dobler's last trip hauling trash-bags out of the room. "While you were up getting clobbered in Diversion, he followed me around like a devoted puppy."

"He had to stay with you," Beowulf said. "You were in a secure government area and he's our assigned escort." He wiped food stains from his face with the warm washcloth Janet had made Dobler fetch from the bathroom she refused to enter.

"Remember he volunteered for that job," Janet said, "and practically drooled all over me the entire afternoon. I know the difference between duty and devotion. For all of his obvious lack of urbane sophistication, Dobler still knows a hot babe when he sees one."

"So I take it that's why you're treating him so severely," Beowulf said. "Bossing him around like you're the armed guards and he's the chain gang."

"Exactly," Janet said. "How dare that little nebbish presume to hope he's actually got a shot with me."

"Oh," Beowulf said. "Actually I assumed you were trying to discourage him by just pretending to be a – what's the modern term – a total bitch?"

"Yeah," Janet said. "That's what I meant. It was all an act."

"I thought so."

"In any case," Janet said, "I brought a change of clothes from your luggage, so we can bust you out of here. All of the federal and military big-wigs are having a meeting in twenty minutes, to discuss the state of the investigation, and I want us to be fully represented there."

Beowulf sat on the edge of his bed and pulled on boxer

shorts and denim slacks, while keeping his hospital gown on, in deference to Janet's presence. "I'm surprised you aren't among the flock of self-important yahoos bleating about how I have to stay in here for a few weeks," he said.

"You forget I was the one assigned by the Institute to recruit you," Janet said. "Like every other assignment, I took it seriously enough to do my homework first. I know everything there is to know about you. In this case I knew how quickly you can recover from any injuries that don't actually kill you." She handed socks, shoes and shirt to the hero, as he needed them.

"What happened to my other clothes?" he said, tying the laces on a pair of worn tennis shoes that had been white, back in a better day.

"What wasn't ripped to shreds by that monster who attacked you, were cut off of you by the emergency room doctors," she said. "Don't worry though. Your precious hat was apparently knocked off early in the fight and was recovered intact." She handed Beowulf the faded brown pilot's cap that had been his visual trademark since the mid-sixties. She'd had it wrapped up in the bundle of clothes.

"And at least that's one nagging mystery solved," she continued, as Beowulf finished dressing. "I finally know why you'd never let anyone see you without that cap on. I know your big secret."

"Oh?" Beowulf said. There may have been a slight flush to his cheeks as he pulled his cap in place.

"A receding hairline is nothing to be embarrassed about," Janet said, clearly enjoying herself. "All the big action heroes have them these days: Bruce Willis; Kevin Costner; and we don't even want to talk about the chrome dome Sean Connery's been trying to hide from the public all these years. So what if you no longer have the full head of glorious night-black hair every young schoolgirl fell in love with back in your glory days?"

"It's not just a matter of vanity," Beowulf said. "I shouldn't have a receding hairline. I shouldn't have a receding anything. For more than a thousand years the dragon's blood has kept me as young as I was the day I bathed in it. Younger in fact. I've looked thirty since that day. It shouldn't be possible for me to lose my hair."

"Unless the power of the dragon's blood is finally beginning to wear off," Janet said.

"Yeah," Beowulf said. "I began to notice.it a few years back. The problem is, if anyone else notices it, they might come to the same conclusion you arrived at so easily. I've made enough enemies during my private hero days that such knowledge might not be in my best interest. Any hint of a weakness and they might start coming out of the woodwork to settle old scores with me. If the blood is wearing off, sooner or later one of them will succeed."

Fully dressed, Beowulf looked around the room to see if he was leaving anything behind. Then he left with Janet to find Dobler.

"I take it my parka was also shredded in the fight," Beowulf said, as they walked down the hospital corridor, trailing a couple of worried National Guardsmen in their wake. They'd been posted outside the room to discourage any mysterious bad guys from coming by to finish the job of killing the once-famous hero. Now that Beowulf was on the move, they weren't entirely sure what to do. It was a crime punishable by hard time in an Army prison to desert ones assigned guard post. Both had been warned what might happen to them if they so much as budged from their place outside of the hero's hospital room. But that presumed Beowulf wouldn't be able to leave it any time soon. Lacking any instructions for this eventuality, they decided their greatest responsibility was to stay with the man they were supposed to protect, all the while praying that their sergeant would see it the same way, once he found out they'd abandoned their post.

"Yes, but I have a new coat for you out in the car," Janet said. "I didn't bring it in with me, because I didn't want to tip off a bunch of meddling doctors that I was about to spring you out of here."

"Is there any chance someone saved those scraps?" Beowulf said.

"Sure. They were all collected back at the hanger," Janet said. "I imagine the forensic sorcerers and scientists want to look at them, just in case what attacked you has some connection to what caused the suicides."

"I think we can be reasonably confident there's a connection," Beowulf said. "We'll need to pick those clothes up, on the way to the big meeting."

"Why?" Janet said.

"I can't tell you," Beowulf said.

"Why not?" Janet said.

"It's a secret," Beowulf said, pantomiming a finger to his lips.

"But I'm the senior partner on this mission," Janet said.

"As you've reminded me on more than one occasion," Beowulf said.

"So you're required to share all plans and information with me," Janet said.

"With you, yes, but not with them," Beowulf said, pointing out their two armed escorts to Janet. "Information about this investigation shall be disseminated strictly on a need to know basis. I believe that's what our written instructions said, right? Security is all."

"Well, you two can leave us alone now," Janet said to the

guards. "We have things to discuss that you can't hear."

"I'm sorry, ma'am," one of the guards said, "but we have to stay with Mister Beowulf. We're his guards."

"Mister Beowulf no longer needs guarding, as you can see for yourselves," Janet said.

"That doesn't matter," Beowulf said, smiling at Janet's frustration. "If I remember my old Army days correctly, one of the standing general orders for every single member of our brave fighting forces is that no one shall quit his post until he's been properly relieved."

"Fine," Janet said. "Then you're both relieved."

"Sorry, ma'am, but you're not in our chain of command, ma'am," the guardsman said.

It was a tight squeeze getting everyone into the compact sedan Janet had rented for their stay in Dillon. Dobler got the worst of it, riding crushed between the two soldiers – and their rifles and bulky combat gear – in the ridiculously tiny rear compartment.

Chapter Eight
State of the Investigation

The meeting started late, after some confusion at the door over who was and wasn't qualified to take part in it. As representatives of the prestigious and – more importantly – well-connected Doctor Pindahl Valentine, Beowulf and Janet Garrow were of course welcome in the meeting. But when the two guardsmen tried to follow Beowulf in, once again citing the relevant general order governing their actions, there was a delay while someone in their direct chain of command could be found to officially relieve them of duty. Following that, there was another uncomfortable moment when the leader of the AWS task force explained to Jeff Dobler that, although he was indeed assigned as liaison to the Saint George Group investigators, that wasn't an important enough job to buy him a seat at the table. There was some whispered conversation between the two AWS agents, about what it means to be low man on the totem pole, and how this meeting was for important grown-up talk, before Dobler, pouting, turned from the door and walked off in a pronounced sulk.

In addition to Janet and Beowulf, a number of important-looking people were seated at the large conference table in the meeting room, part of a cluster of office buildings that, like the hanger across the tarmac, had been requisitioned from the Dillon airport for the huge, secret investigation. After all the coffee was poured and all the briefcases had been opened, the meeting finally got underway.

"Good morning, ladies and gentlemen," a full-bird Army colonel said, far down the table from where Beowulf and Janet were seated. "For those of you who've recently joined this investigation, I'm Colonel Bill MacCauley, from the US Army Sorcery Support Command. We'll begin with update reports from each of the department heads. Medical Forensics?"

"We may have pinned down something," Gil Franklin, from the Center for Disease Control said. "Each body seems to be contaminated with a rare substance derived from the sap of the upas tree. The upas sap is extremely poisonous and – more importantly – highly potent in raw magical energy. As our friend from the AWS can no doubt tell us, upas extract is often used in the creation of some of the more deadly alchemical potions."

"So these people were poisoned with this upas sap?" Colonel MacCauley said.

"No, the concentration was too small." Franklin said. "If upas extract was used as a direct poison, none of the victims would have lived long enough to commit suicide. In this case we believe the extract was used as the active magic ingredient in whatever the potion was designed to do. In a sense, it was the battery that powered the metaphorical engine, but we still don't know what the engine, the other active ingredients in our presumed potion, were."

"That's some headway at least," Colonel MacCauley said. "If our X-Bug is an alchemical agent, that rules out a biological or mundane chemical agent, right? That narrows the scope of our investigations considerably. Congratulations, Doctor Franklin. Good work."

"Actually the credit in this case belongs to our friends from the Valentine Group," Franklin said. "Miss Garrow passed some of our data along to Doctor Kacirk in their Forensic Sorcery department. She was the one who pinned down the upas presence that I, and everyone in my team, missed completely."

Like a miniature sports-stadium "wave," nods of congratulation rippled down the table towards Janet, who positively beamed from the attention she received from the assembled luminaries, finally giving her the recognition Beowulf had been stealing.

"Any chance this upas contamination could be a natural occurrence?" Tom Archer said. He was the senior AWS man – the one who'd kicked Dobler out of the meeting. Contrary to what Gil Franklin supposed, he'd had no idea that upas extract was a common ingredient in certain types of magic potions. He was a longtime government bureaucrat, not a scientist. "Diversion is surrounded by all kinds of trees. Hell, it sits in the middle of a damned forest that stretches from Canada to Mexico."

"No chance of that," Franklin said. "The upas tree is isolated to two or three sites in Indonesia, and so rare that a thimble full of extract costs more than the combined annual salary of everyone in this room. Whatever this thing was, it didn't show up naturally. Whether by accident or on purpose, this substance was introduced."

"Then we need to find out how your upas potion was introduced and we'll be getting somewhere," Colonel MacCauley said. "That's were we need to concentrate."

"Actually we already know that," Beowulf said, surprising everyone around the table, most specifically Janet, who realized in a sudden intuitive epiphany that he was about to steal her thunder once again. The old hero pulled a few folded and crumpled pieces of lined paper from one pocket, and smoothed the pages out on the table in front of him. "These were what I needed to retrieve from the shreds of my coat," he said in an aside to Janet. Then, to the rest of the room, he continued, "I found these pages in the daily incident blotter in Diversion's police station. Mixed in with the records of traffic tickets issued, and drunks arrested, are several notations that reveal how the suicide potion was purposefully introduced to the town."

Beowulf had the rapt and silent attention of everyone in the room, as he read the brief notations of a small-town marshal, whose body lay a hundred yards away, contorted in the position it was frozen in, after he'd blown his head off with a 10-gauge shotgun.

"Saturday, January 5, 12:40 pm," Beowulf read. "Some sort of smoke bomb, dropped out of a small plane, landed in Ned Bauer's yard. Red smoke all over Bauer, Powell and Williams property. No injuries. Prank?

"Sunday, January 6, 10:00 pm. Another two smoke bombs. Small plane, same description. Same plane? Green smoke landed in schoolyard. No injuries. Red smoke landed in Henry's horse field. No injuries.

"Tuesday, January 8, 2:15 pm. Our mad smoke bomber is back. Monday his day off? Red smoke hit Bob Olney's roof and rolled off. No fire. No injuries. Green smoke landed in treeline west edge of town. Frank Mellon says these are old military surplus smoke grenades. No injuries."

Beowulf went on to read another two week's worth of police blotter entries which chronicled the almost daily visits of the town's so-called "mad bomber." No one was ever hurt, though the number of complaints from the townspeople increased day by day. In the final week the bombing raids settled down to one smoke grenade a day, which was dropped in a grass field west of Diversion, where the prevailing winds would blow the colored smoke so that it spread through the entire town.

"After that there are no more bombing incidents for the eight days prior to the last blotter entry," Beowulf finished.

"Which is the day everyone decided to kill themselves,"

A woman in a white lab coat said.

"From the evidence Mister Beowulf just presented, we can conclude that someone was testing the local wind conditions, before finally dropping his killer gas bomb," Colonel MacCauley said. "He – whoever he is – wanted to make sure his gas would spread through the entire town, before it dissipated."

"And he finally knew a bomb dropped in that grass field on the west side would do the trick," Beowulf said, "but kept testing it for a few days to make sure. Our killer doesn't leave things to chance. I found the military smoke grenades that were used for the testing phase. They were all in a cardboard box, in the police station. But the actual suicide bomb wasn't there."

"No, it wouldn't be," Gil Franklin said. "Because there would be no one left alive to go collect that one."

"Why is this the first time we're seeing this information?" Colonel MacCauley barked towards an Army captain, seated midway down the table. "Your team was responsible for collecting physical evidence, Captain Warner."

"Both the marshal and his deputy killed themselves well away from the police station," Warner said, knowing that the excuse wouldn't save him. "Since we found no bodies in the station, it didn't occur to us that there was any evidence to be found there."

"Now I guess you know different, Captain," Colonel MacCauley said. "If your men had done their jobs correctly, we'd have saved a week to ten days' work. Do you care to guess what that delay cost the taxpayers?"

Captain Warner didn't care to guess, and was saved, for the moment, by Doctor Franklin's interruption. "What we need to do immediately is find the actual bomb. It's the key to this mystery. It will be some kind of small canister or other container, with a capacity similar to the volume of one of those smoke grenades. If we can find it, we can test it in a hundred ways that may reveal what sort of potion it was and who made it."

"There's only two possible places it could be," Captain Warner said. "It's either among the physical artifacts we've already collected, or it's still in that field." Warner dearly hoped it would be found among the items already collected. Failing to find two vital pieces of evidence would surely be the end of his career.

"Assuming that creature that attacked me wasn't up there to get it first," Beowulf said.

"That would explain what it was doing there," Janet said, glad to finally be able to contribute to the conversation. "Our unknown enemy couldn't have known Beowulf would be part of the investigation, since he's been in retirement for decades. The public doesn't know yet that he's back in business. So we have to conclude that the monster was up there on some other errand and Beowulf was just a target of opportunity."

Beowulf knew better, but didn't say so out loud. The red monster's single statement to him, "You should have stayed in retirement," revealed that it knew he was in Diversion, and was obviously sent there to kill him. Janet was right that very few people could know he'd come out of retirement; only those conducting this investigation, or the members of the Institute that had so recently recruited him. Somewhere among the two groups, here or in Philadelphia, there was a traitor feeding information to the enemy. Since the list of suspects also included everyone in the room, Beowulf remained silent.

Thankfully, for Captain Warner's career at least, the suicide bomb was found among the artifacts collected from Diversion. It was an aluminum canister eight inches long and three inches across, topped by a small gas-release device designed along the same lines as those on the military surplus smoke grenades that had been used to test it.

After its discovery things moved quickly.

Scrapings from the inside of the canister were tested by the arcane machines and chemicals of a dozen different science and sorcery departments. Less than 24 hours after the canister was identified the alchemy team had worked out a rough approximation of the suicide gas formula, only on paper of course; an actual reproduction of the potion, if desired at all, would require weeks of work and a number of ingredients stockpiled in only a very few places on this world.

Every bit of the exterior surface of the canister was tested for latent fingerprints, before sending it to other departments for metallurgy and fabrication tests on the metal parts; chemical analysis of the epoxy that was used to seal both end-caps of the container – which would also be examined for hairs or fibers, that tend to stick to adhesives, no matter how much subsequent cleaning the item is subjected to; magnified visual examination for toolmarks and fabricator's marks; composition analysis of each individual part of the gas-spraying mechanism; and a series of detailed tests for any other types of foreign residue.

The fingerprint tests produced five good sets, clear enough for possible identification. Four of the five sets were found to have come from members of the combined investigation group. They were quickly and routinely ruled out as possible subjects of the investigation after interviews with those individuals determined the circumstances under which each had handled the item, from the female Army private who'd first taken it out of the field west of Diversion, to lowly Jeff Dobler, who'd helped sort the physical evidence, prior to being assigned as a liaison to the two Saint George Group field agents.

That left them with one unidentified subject.

The unidentified print was faxed to the FBI's Criminal Justice Information Services center in Clarksburg, Virginia, where it was given top priority. The FBI's massive 640 million dollar fingerprint identification database contained the equivalent of 34 million print cards within its memory, which increased by 50 thousand new print files each day. It took exactly seven minutes and thirty-six seconds to match the print to Edward Kilmer of Wisdom, Montana, who owned and operated a one-man air charter service out of that same town. Kilmer had no criminal record, nor was he wanted for any crime. He'd been fingerprinted as a condition of employment in a small passenger airline service, before quitting to start his own company.

Chapter Nine
Wisdom

Wisdom was located less than fifty miles northwest of Dillon. Within thirty minutes of Kilmer's identification, FBI agents, AWS agents and two squads of heavily armed Army Rangers, trained in small-unit urban warfare, climbed aboard a pair of Army Black Hawk helicopters which already had their rotors turning on the tarmac. While the two helicopters were in flight, high over the Pioneer Mountains, the exact location – accurate within one meter – of the Kilmer Air Service office was uploaded to their onboard global navigation system computers. 23 minutes after liftoff, the helicopters touched down outside of the Kilmer Air Service building, which turned out to be a roughly rectangular patch of black soot and ash on the tarmac of Wisdom's tiny airport. A few isolated black charcoal timbers and half-melted pipes stuck up out of the destroyed area. Otherwise it was featureless.

"Place burned down two days ago," an old man said. He'd shuffled up to the forbidding team of icy-nerved gunmen that had fanned out from the two aircraft, even before they had fully touched down. "What did poor Eddie do to piss off so many people?" The old man was bald, with little more than a pencil-line of white hair over his ears and around the back of his deeply wrinkled head. He wore a child's yellow rain slicker over a huge dirty wool sweater that hung below his knees. As soon as he spoke, a dozen guns were turned to train on the man, who didn't seem afraid, or even particularly aware of the possible danger.

"Why? Who else did Mister Kilmer anger?" John Bristol,

one of the FBI agents, said, after it seemed likely none of the Rangers was going to accidentally shoot the old man dead.

"The Mutt and Jeff who killed him," the old man said. "They drove up in their panel truck in the middle of the night, with their headlights dark. Then the big one, an Indian feller, carries Eddie over his shoulder, like a sack of 'taters. Dumps him in his office while the little guy is splashing gasoline all over the place. Then the big guy comes out alone and they set fire to it. While that starts going, they drive out to Eddie's plane and do the same thing to it, only no body goes in first. Then they drive off, slick as you please."

"You saw all of this?" Bristol said.

"Sure as taxes," the old man said. "No one's supposed to be here at night, so I guess them fellers thought they'd be able to do their dirty deeds with no one to see, but I saw. I sweep up for Ben Randall's outfit over there, and some nights the last bus stops running before I'm done. I guess I've slowed down some. On those nights, Mister Randall lets me bunk in the machine shop, right under the window that looks over where this shack used to be. Only I don't sleep so well some nights and on that night I was awake to see the whole damned thing."

"I don't suppose you got the license number of the van they drove," Bristol said.

"Bet your smooth as a baby turtle's ass I did. Some guys dump a body and start lighting fires all over the damned place, and I jump to all sorts of conclusions, like maybe there's a crime in progress. So I scribbled it down."

The old man shuffled back to the enclosed small aircraft hanger and attached offices that were labeled King of the Mountains Charter Air Service, to get the license number. A flying wedge of soldiers and law enforcement officers trailed in his wake.

"Who investigated the fires?" Bristol said, as they walked.

"Our no-account sheriff," the old man said.

"Has he traced the license number yet?"

"I doubt it, since I didn't give it to him."

"Why not?"

"Because I ain't said one civil word to that goose-stepping brownshirt punk, since he wrote me out a ten dollar ticket back in nineteen and sixty three, just because I let my dog Rex drop his mail where he's been doing it since before mighty Sheriff Loumen was nothing more than his mother's nasty thought."

The old man, whose name turned out to be Larry, found the license number, where he'd written in on the corner of a calendar in the machine shop. On their way out of the building, Bristol paused, remembering another question he meant to ask.

"You said you thought one of the men was an Indian," he asked Larry. "Was that an American Indian, or an East Indian?"

"American," Larry said.

"How did you know that?" Bristol said.

"How do you think? The guy wore feathers, warpaint and moccasins, and danced all around the fire he lit, going 'woo woo woo,' and then, before he left, he came over to me and sold me the entire island of Manhattan for a few glass beads. Naw, pick your jaw up off the floor, sonny. I'm just pulling your leg. I could see he was an Indian because he was a big red-skinned feller."

Chapter Ten
Someone at the Door

Janet Garrow was livid. Beowulf had shown her up again, and it was past time to work out a few basic protocols for the remainder of their field assignment. She pounded on his hotel room door, and then paused, waiting for him to answer. She could hear him inside the room, but he never answered the door. She pounded harder and longer.

Inside the room Beowulf was on the phone, long distance to the Institute.

"What's that noise?" Pindahl Valentine said. His voice came flat and distant over the receiver.

"I think it's Janet," Beowulf said. "Her room's next door and my guess is she's entertaining. She's found herself a new friend and thinks he's the cat's pajamas."

"Good for her. I hope it works out," Valentine said. "Janet deserves to find some happiness in this world, if it's still possible. How are you two getting on together?"

"Rippingly."

"Good. Glad to hear it," Valentine said. "Now, as far as your inquiries go, our database has nothing resembling the type of creature you've described. It's likely we have a new monster here. New to us anyway."

"So you've designated it in the official monster class already?" Beowulf said.

"Based on what you reported – what it was able to do to you – it was an easy call to make," Valentine said. "Your Red Monster hits the charts at number 47, with a bullet, bumping everyone else down a notch. Destroy it if you can, but above all be careful."

"Thanks, I'll try to do that."

"And please pass on my best regards to Janet. I knew you two would work well together."

"I'll do that too."

Beowulf let Janet into his room, after hanging up the phone. She stomped in, her body language showing every bit of the fury she felt.

"We need to talk," she said.

"No, we don't," Beowulf said. "Unless you're here for a remedial course in basic manners. I was already getting tired of your huffing and puffing over the last few days, every time I had the presumption to speak up, without asking your permission first. The door-pounding put you over the top."

"I'm the senior partner," she said. "You should defer to me."

"I've never been the deferential type, Miss Garrow. For all of your research into my history, I'm surprised that character trait managed to slip by you."

"In order for a field investigation to run smoothly, each party needs to stick to his or her area of responsibility. You are muscle. You were sent here to do the heavy lifting and watch my back. You shouldn't have been up in Diversion, sifting for clues like some amateur sleuth. I'm the trained investigator."

"Let me point out to you a few things wrong with your pretty little theories," Beowulf said. "First, I hate anyone who uses 'his or her' in a sentence. Pick one. Second, regardless of how you've pigeon-holed me in your mind as little more than a thug-for-hire, I'm also an experienced investigator, with more years on the job than you have coming to you in your entire life. Use your head, Miss Garrow, do you think I've been just one thing for as long as I've been alive? I've been around for centuries, and had hundreds of careers. I've been a chef and a surgeon and an international jewel thief. I've been a bomber pilot, and conducted police investigations, and taken every other job that's struck my fancy. No immortal remains in one profession for more than a hundred years or so. Finally, you've carefully left out the fact that it was my snooping around up in Diversion that blew this case wide open."

"You may have been all those things in the past," Janet said, "but let us both recall that when I found you, you were a smelly drunk in a one-room ghetto apartment."

"Which I've been on more than one occasion," he said. "Some social scientist at the University of Coventry posits a condition he calls Immortal's Funk, or Fugue, or something like that; the basic idea being that those of us who are here for the long count have necessary times where we aren't exactly the movers and shakers of the world. We need these occasional unproductive downtimes where we take menial, uninvolving jobs, while we recharge the batteries, or cleanse the palate, or whatever other metaphor suits you. I suspect he may be on to something. For the last few years, before you stumbled into my life, I've been a bouncer at a bar you won't find on this world, a day laborer, and the guy who delivers groceries from the local market. But so what? I've also in my time been an oceanographer, a theoretical mathematician and a super hero. Do you really want to compare resumes with me? Or maybe we should skip all this preliminary nonsense and jump right to where we pull our pants down to see whose dick is longer?"

"You are a vulgar man," Janet said. "I don't like you very much."

"And yet you tried so hard to recruit me."

"I was against hiring you, but I don't run the Institute.

Once Doctor Valentine overruled my objections, I did everything I could to convince you to join us, because that was my job, and I always do my job well."

"I'm so glad to hear that," Beowulf said, "because right now your job is to get out of my room, and find your way over to your own room, with a minimum of screaming, whining or door slamming. We have an early day tomorrow and I'd like to get a few hours sleep first."

Janet Garrow got little sleep that night, tossing and turning in profound frustration. When she heard the quiet knock on her hotel room door at a little past four in the morning, she assumed Beowulf had finally come over to apologize. She was very wrong.

Chapter Eleven
Traces of Brimstone

After Janet failed to meet Dobler and him in the hotel restaurant for breakfast, Beowulf called her room and got no answer. Then he went back up to their floor and knocked on her door for a while. Then he found a maid with a passkey. Once the room was opened the maid couldn't stop screaming.

Hours later, outside the Dillon airport hanger, Beowulf had a private conversation with Colonel MacCauley, commander of the combined investigation force. They walked together along one of the airplane taxiways, in the cold drizzling rain.

"The medical examiners said she put up quite a fight," MacCauley said. "She had defensive wounds all over her hands and arms." He wore his regulation long gray raincoat over his uniform, and smoked a long, chocolate-brown cigar.

"And that red stuff they scraped from under her nails?" Beowulf said.

"Brimstone," MacCauley said. "Can you believe it?"

"Actually that makes a certain kind of sense," Beowulf said. "Was she raped first?"

"That's impossible to tell, considering the degree of dismemberment. What makes you ask?" The smoke from his cigar mixed with their breath vapor in the cold air.

"The word 'whore' was written in her blood on the wall," Beowulf said. "That seems to imply a sexual component to the murder."

"Maybe when all the lab work comes back, we'll know

more," MacCauley said. "But for all we're uncovering on this case, I feel like we're falling farther and farther behind. That pilot's body was a dead end. His filed flight-plans don't include trips to Diversion, but their times match up with the flyovers reported in that cop's police journal. Fuel purchases match what it would take to make the round-trip flights from Wisdom to Diversion. So we're sure he's the one who dropped the suicide bomb on Diversion. But we didn't find anything linking him to the construction of the device."

"Meaning he was just a hired gun," Beowulf said.

"Yeah, and in the last 24 hours we've been through every piece of paperwork he generated in his life, but he didn't leave a thing behind to finger whoever hired him. Dead end. Our real enemy covered his tracks well."

Every minute or two, a jet or propeller plane accelerated down the runway that paralleled the taxiway along which they walked. The planes took off with a roar of powerful engines, trailing clouds of jet exhaust and water vapor behind them.

"I think it's time we discussed what we do know," Beowulf said. "And what you had to have guessed by now. No one had anything against anyone in the town of Diversion, did they? They were picked maybe randomly of off a map; killed because they were a nicely contained small population, remote enough to make them a good test group."

"Yeah, that's about what I figure," MacCauley said. They'd reached the far end of the airplane taxiway and turned to walk back to the hanger.

"Which means that our quarry is building a weapon," Beowulf said. "In fact he's completed the weapon, and probably finished testing it. Maybe the focus of your investigation should expand to include finding out what he intends to do with it, now that he knows it works."

"Oh, I think we know that already," MacCauley said. "He

wants to get rich, and unless we find him soon, he's going to succeed. A battlefield weapon that makes your enemy lose hope and kill themselves? Any nation in the world would pay out the nose to have such a thing in their arsenal. Hell, because it doesn't directly kill the targets, it doesn't even strictly violate the international conventions against lethal gasses. Our own military could use it, until new laws were written to close the loophole. It's practically perfect."

"Then his recent actions don't make much sense," Beowulf said. "If he's already got his weapon, why kill Janet and try to kill me? It gains him nothing. In fact, assuming he covered his tracks well enough – which he seems to have done, he should want this investigation to go forward. It would even be in his interest to help it. When the time comes to sell his goods, the results we've uncovered should be wonderful independent verification of his weapon's effectiveness. Why try to stop us while we're handing him a fortune in free promotion?"

"Who knows?" MacCauley said. "Maybe he has a particular grudge against you and Agent Garrow. That creature that attacked you up in Diversion could've picked off my soldiers up there with ease, but it left them alone. Since he's only attacked you two, and since you two are the only two agents here from the Saint George Group, maybe he has some nut against your Institute. Or maybe that creature isn't actually connected to our weapons maker after all."

"Too much of a coincidence," Beowulf said. "I don't buy it."

"Naw, neither do I," MacCauley said. "So, what's your next step?" He stamped out the stub of his dark cigar on the wet tarmac.

"One I've been putting off," Beowulf said. "I have to call Doctor Valentine and let him know I've completely failed to do my job, getting Janet Garrow killed as a result."

They split up. Colonel MacCauley walked past the security perimeter of National Guard soldiers, back into the hanger, to resume directing the investigation. Beowulf went in search of a private place with a phone.

•

"I'm very disappointed in you," Doctor Valentine said, from over the phone.

"You and me both," Beowulf said. He was in one of the several offices that the combined investigation force had commandeered from the Dillon Public Airport.

"You're developing a habit of letting women die while under your protection," Valentine said. "First the young St. Clair woman and now Miss Garrow. The first incident cost you your hero's license in Coventry. Can you provide me any good reason why this incident shouldn't cost you your position in this Institute, and thus your new Pennsylvania hero's license?"

"Not offhand."

"Then I should call you home, and send either Prester John or William Churchill to replace you, as soon as one of them becomes available." Valentine's cultured voice never varied in volume. He was a man in control of his passions.

"That's your prerogative," Beowulf said, "but orders to the contrary or no, I won't be returning; not until I've tracked down the Red Monster, and destroyed it, after first forcing it to identify its partner, or master; whatever their relationship turns out to be."

"I was warned you had tendencies toward insubordination."

"You should have heeded that warning," Beowulf said.

"Perhaps," Valentine said. Then after a long moment of silence he continued, "You'll have a better chance of success if you still have the official support of the Institute. So you may continue with the mission. But let me be clear, Mister Beowulf, I want the Red Monster and the other one destroyed. I want Janet Garrow fully avenged. Nothing less will be considered satisfactory."

"I understand," Beowulf said, and hung up the phone.

As he stepped once more into the drizzling rain, out from the cluster of small offices, Beowulf encountered Colonel MacCauley, Jeff Dobler, and more than a dozen grim-faced well-armed soldiers. None of the soldiers had their rifles aimed directly at him. Not quite.

Chapter Twelve
The Available Evidence

"Were you and Agent Garrow involved in a sexual relationship?" Colonel MacCauley asked. His face was a cold block of stone. The soldiers behind him were fanned out in a semi-circle, curving around Beowulf as its center of focus. Their assault rifles were held at the ready.

"None of your business," Beowulf said.

"She spent time in your hotel room last night, before returning to her own. Did you have sex with her then?" MacCauley said.

"Once again, that's none of your business," Beowulf said, "but I'd like to know how you knew her movements last night."

"She was seen by a witness," MacCauley said. Beowulf looked at Dobler, who suddenly had trouble meeting his gaze.

"Why don't you get to the point, Colonel?" Beowulf said. "What's this all about?" He forced his voice to remain calm, but a fire of ancient anger was building inside him.

"The medical examiners recovered semen from the body of Agent Garrow. We tested it immediately and it came back with interesting results. The blood of the man who secreted that semen is contaminated with dragon's blood."

"That is surprising," Beowulf said. He put his hands in the pockets of his coat to warm them.

"Please keep your hands in sight, sir," one of the soldiers, a staff sergeant, said. His tone was polite, but the muzzle of his weapon, a 12-gauge military assault shotgun, drifted closer towards being aimed at the old hero.

"I don't know anyone on this earth, other than you, whose blood would be contaminated with dragon's blood," MacCauley said. "Do you?"

"No," Beowulf said. "As far as I know, I'm unique in that regard." He slowly removed his hands from the pockets of his coat, and let them hang in plain sight by his sides.

"Now I've explained why your sexual activities are my business," MacCauley said. "So now I expect you to answer my question, without any more crap. Did you have sexual intercourse with Agent Garrow last night?"

"No," Beowulf said. "Not last night and not ever."

"Then we seem to have a problem," MacCauley said. "I'm placing you under apprehension, pending a criminal investigation." The drizzle turned into a full rainfall, and the heavy, falling drops seemed to force each of the soldiers' muzzles down, until they were all trained directly on Beowulf's chest.

"What is there to investigate?" Beowulf said. "I'll provide a blood sample for DNA testing against your semen evidence, and the thing will be resolved."

"There's also the matter of the reported hostility between you and Miss Garrow," MacCauley said.

"According to who?" Beowulf said, noticing that young Dobler looked even more embarrassed than he had moments before.

"I'm sorry, Mister Beowulf. I'm real sorry," Dobler said, "but Janet told me how mad she was at you for constantly going behind her back. When this happened – when she was found murdered – I had no choice but to report it. I had to."

Beowulf allowed himself to be taken into custody, even though Colonel MacCauley seriously underestimated the number of men and weapons it would take to subdue him, had he decided to resist. They placed him in handcuffs he could have snapped with a single flex of his wrists, and read him the version of his Miranda rights that apply to those under the authority of the Uniform Code of Military Justice. Strictly speaking, Beowulf could be considered under military authority while part of the combined investigation.

He was transported, via Army sedan, into the city of Dillon, to their city jail. Once there, they locked him in the one spell-reinforced detention cell they had, which had been designed for the incarceration of supernatural subjects. Beowulf suspected he could have broken out easily. Instead he unrolled the thin mattress on the metal shelf that served as a bunk, and stretched out for a nap.

Three hours after he was first locked up, a medic came to take a blood sample. The medic was accompanied by two armed guards and a man in an expensive business suit who had Beowulf sign several forms to record that he was willingly turning over his blood, even though it could be used in evidence against him. Everyone was suitably deferential, and one of the guards even apologized for his part in the process, and left with Beowulf's autograph on an old paperback book detailing one of his fictional adventures.

Dinner arrived shortly afterwards; rotelli pasta, with tomato sauce, hot Italian sausage, and garlic bread. It was surprisingly good, even if the portions were less than what he was accustomed to. The guard who picked up his used tray and utensils – carefully checking that both fork and spoon were present – dropped off a bag of magazines and paperback books, sent to him by Jeff Dobler. The guard took the plastic bag with him when he left, in case Beowulf might attempt to use it to commit suicide. Earlier, they had already removed his belt, shoelaces and cap for the same reasons. He'd passed a good hour of his time by idly trying to dream up some way in which he could possibly kill himself with his worn old pilot's cap. Stab himself repeatedly with the brass wolf-head insignia pin perhaps?

At ten o'clock that evening, the light in his cell was shut off automatically. In the sudden dark, he folded down the page to mark his place in the book – a science fiction tale about soldiers in the future who fought in atomic-powered suits of battle armor – and undressed down to his shorts, before stretching out to sleep again.

Late into the night he was awoken by the series of metallic clanks that proceeded the opening of his cell door. A bright light stabbed him in the eyes, from the direction of the doorway.

"What now?" Beowulf said, squinting to see past the light.

"Mister Beowulf? Come on, you're free to go."

"Who is that?" Beowulf said. "Get that light out of my eyes."

"Oh, sorry. It's me, Jeff Dobler." The light moved out of Beowulf's eyes and focused briefly on the man holding it, before moving to shine on the floor, midway between the two of them. It was indeed Dobler standing there, badly dressed in a too-large prison guard's uniform.

"What the hell are you doing here, Dobler?" Beowulf sat up, wiping the sleep from his eyes.

"I'm busting you out of here, Mister Beowulf," Dobler said. "Hurry up and get dressed. I'm not sure how long our knockout-gas will keep the guards asleep."

"I'm not busting out," Beowulf said. "Don't be ridiculous, you damned fool kid. By tomorrow they'll know my blood doesn't match their sample and I'll be out of here legitimately."

"That's not going to happen, sir," Dobler said. "They've already done the preliminary tests. Your blood matched the sample close enough that they're preparing formal charges against you."

"Nonsense. That's not possible."

"I believe that you didn't do it," Dobler said, "but someone did a good job so far, framing you for the crime. Hurry up, now. We have to get going."

"I told you I'm not going anywhere," Beowulf said.

"Damn it but you can be an uncooperative pain in the ass," Dobler said. "I'd hoped to be able to do this elsewhere." Then he drew an odd looking gun out of the guard's holster he wore and shot Beowulf three times, in the chest, neck and face respectively.

Chapter Thirteen
Blood Relations

Beowulf woke slowly to the thwop thwoping sound of overhead helicopter rotors, muffled by the insulation and partial soundproofing of the aircraft's cabin. He had a pounding headache that kept rhythm with the turning of the rotor blades. Its pain grew as his comprehension grew, rising with him as he rose slowly into consciousness, flooding to fill each space, as he became aware of it.

He found himself lying on the deck of a large interior cabin, that vibrated with the force of powerful engines. His first impression was that he was wrapped tightly in a heavy, cold and horribly lumpy blanket. As his wits returned he realized they were chains, several different lengths of chain, wrapped around him so thoroughly that all but his head and feet were entirely enclosed in a bulky cocoon of dull gray links. He could make out a number of padlocks of various sizes and vintages that secured the chains confining him. He looked like nothing so much as a cartoon caricature of the helpless victim in a TV melodrama.

Straining the mobility of his neck to its limit, he could make out most of the cabin in which he lay. From the familiar sound of the rotors and engines, and the configuration of the cabin space, including the cargo loading door at the rear of the compartment, he guessed that he was in a CH-53 Sea Stallion helicopter, one of the more reliable workhorses of the American military for the past thirty years. He'd ridden in many of these craft over the last three decades, but never before bound as he was.

BILL WILLINGHAM

He wasn't alone in the cabin. Seated on benches, bolted along one bulkhead, Beowulf recognized Jeff Dobler and the Red Monster. The Red Monster looked much as it did the last time Beowulf encountered it. Its gray overcoat was ripped in a few places, which was the closet he'd come to damaging the creature in their recent battle. It sat motionless, the way only something not truly alive can sit. Dobler was dressed in a green one-piece overall, similar to that worn by any member of a military flight-crew. Over the flight-suit he wore an inflatable survival vest of the type worn by one conducting flight operations away from land. Dobler no longer looked like the eager and innocent young man he'd appeared to be over the past few days. Though his features were the same, they were now composed in a way that suggested dark intelligence, and a complete lack of anything resembling innocence.

"You're a hard man to kill," Dobler said, after he was certain Beowulf was fully awake. "Those darts I shot you with were full of enough nerve agent to instantly kill a hundred men. But they just put you to sleep for a few days."

"Why are we headed out to sea?" Beowulf said. His voice sounded like someone had been at his throat with a wood-rasp. He tasted dried blood in his mouth.

"Bravo," Dobler said, and pantomimed polite applause. "The mighty hero is also a detective worthy of Philip Marlowe and Sherlock Holmes. How did you work that out so quickly? You can't see out of the windows from down there. Was it the faint smell of salt sea air?"

"Nothing so clever as all that," Beowulf said. "You're wearing a life vest, and there's a sea survival raft strapped near the door over there that's not standard equipment on this model of helicopter. It's one of those deluxe, sheltered and powered things, normally available only on the more ritzy

79

passenger ships."

"What can I say?" Dobler said. "I'm a nervous flyer. As to why we're headed out to sea, that's for your benefit. After failing to kill you twice, I'm concerned that it may not be possible to kill you. So I plan to dump you far out to sea, where you will sink into the darkest depths and continue to live uncomfortably until the end of time, as far as I care."

"And is this some personal vendetta against me, or was I simply in your way?"

"Call it a little of both."

"Care to explain why?" Beowulf said. "How does a low-level civil servant get involved in the creation and trafficking of lethal magic weapons?"

"I've never actually worked in any government agency," Dobler said. "The real AWS Agent, Jeff Dobler who left from Baltimore, Maryland, was not the same Jeff Dobler who arrived in Montana, to join the combined investigation force. Sooner or later someone will open the airport locker that contains his dismembered body in two matched suitcases."

"And you took Dobler's place to keep an eye on how the investigation was going?" Beowulf said.

"Exactly. The amount of information I was able to obtain, on how well my suicide gas worked, is priceless. I have copies of everything right here, along with the original formulas, manufacturing specifications, and two remaining prototypes of my invention." The false Dobler patted a silver-colored metal briefcase strapped securely to the legs of the passenger bench. "The independent scientific data our investigation team generated will allow me to double the price I demand."

"You're a clever sorcerer for one so young," Beowulf said.

"I'm not nearly as young as I look," he said. "I haven't

been around as long as you, but let's just say I've looked this young for more than one human lifespan. And I'm not much of a sorcerer, either. My talents lie more in the inspiration and administration fields. I had the ideas, but not the skills to realize them. So I assembled the team of scientists and sorcerers who created both the suicide weapon, and my faithful, and very useful, companion here." He gestured at the Red Monster that continued to sit still, like a lifeless statue.

"And will those scientists and sorcerers get to share in the rewards generated by their work?" Beowulf said.

"Alas, no" Dobler said – Beowulf couldn't help but still think of him by the name he'd become used to. "They have each suffered unfortunate and fatal accidents, over the last few weeks. I'll simply have to enjoy my life as a multi-billionaire all that more vigorously, as a living tribute to their cherished memories."

"So that stuff in your briefcase is the only existing record of how to create your suicide gas?" Beowulf said.

"Oh dear, Mister Beowulf, have you been pumping me for information?" Dobler looked delighted. "What were you planning to do, roll over here and gnaw the case loose with your teeth, and then what – eat it to keep civilization safe? That's marvelous."

"Maybe not that, precisely," Beowulf said, "but I was hoping to figure something out."

"A hero to the end."

"Better than just lying here, waiting for you to roll me out the back door," Beowulf said. "So what's the story on your creature there? It's been some time since anything smaller than a main battle tank has been able to give me so much trouble."

"He's quite remarkable, isn't he? I had him created specifically to be able to destroy you someday. It was an unexpected but welcome surprise to have you walk into the middle of this operation and save me the trouble of coming after you later. He's a golem, constructed out of brimstone, purchased at great cost from the lowest pits of Hell. It's the same material that was used to build Satan's infernal throne. It took me more than a century to close that deal. I call my monster Hellstone for just that reason."

"Too bad the devil ripped you off," Beowulf said. "From what I hear, that stuff's so heavy that this machine could never lift it. We'd never have gotten off the ground if your so-called Hellstone creature was made of actual infernal-grade brimstone."

"Normally that would be true," Dobler said, "but the same magic fuel that powers Hellstone's pseudo-life also powers the partial levitation spells that cancel most of his weight. He was my life's work for many years. I wouldn't have accepted inferior materials."

"What sort of magic fuel would that be?" Beowulf said.

"Haven't you figured that out yet?" Dobler said. "I'm terribly disappointed in you, sir. I withdraw my earlier comparison of you to the great detectives. All the clues have been dangling before you, in plain sight, for days. He's powered by the one substance that could absolutely guarantee he'd have the strength to best you in a fight. Dragon's blood."

"I don't believe it," Beowulf said. "There haven't been confirmed dragons on this world since…"

"Since the one you killed so many centuries past?" Dobler said. "As far as I know, that's correct. There are no more living dragons. So where do you suppose I found a reliable supply of it?"

"I couldn't begin to guess," Beowulf said.

"From my own veins," Dobler said. "Like you, my blood is permanently contaminated with the blood of a dragon –

specifically the same dragon that infected you. I perfected a technique for distilling the pure dragon's blood from my own. It's very costly, painful and time consuming. It took me four decades to produce the amount of dragon's blood Hellstone burned up in that one battle with you, up in Diversion. He was almost bone dry by the time those soldiers showed up and drove him away with their ridiculous guns and grenades."

"The fireworks I thought I heard," Beowulf said.

"If Hellstone had just a thimble-full more blood in him, those toys would never have been able to harm him. As it was, he was nearly immobile by the time he reached safety. I had just enough additional distilled dragon's blood in supply to revive him, and keep him going for a few more weeks, provided he doesn't have to fight something like you again."

"Then what do you do?" Beowulf said. "Park him in the garage for another forty years, until you can process enough juice for another fill-up?"

"No, I've found an alternate supply of dragon-contaminated blood," Dobler said.

"Me?" Beowulf said.

"No, not you," Dobler replied. A wave of undisguised hate crossed over his features. "Even to keep Hellstone alive, I wouldn't forgo my revenge on you. I still plan to dump you in the middle of the ocean."

"Why?" Beowulf said. "As far as I know, we've never met. What could I have done to make you want revenge against me?"

"Can the famous hero actually be such a complete dullard?" Dobler said. "Can you be so blind to the only possible explanation? Ask yourself this: How could my blood be contaminated with dragon's blood, just like yours? How could my semen sample, deposited in that whore's foul cunny, pass as a match for yours, in a high enough percentage of comparison points, that you would be arrested for her murder?"

"Oh dear god," Beowulf said, realizing the truth at last. "We're related."

"That's right, daddy," Dobler said. "I'm your beloved son."

The unceasing thwop thwop, metronome sound of the rotors continued, as the Sea Stallion helicopter flew ever farther out to sea.

Chapter Fourteen
Children of the Dragon

"You're my son?" Beowulf said. Chained aboard Dobler's helicopter, resignation had replaced the tone of surprise that had first colored his voice.

"One of many," Dobler said. "How many sons and daughters did you imagine you might have out there, daddy? Did you ever even take a single moment out of your important life to consider it? Lord knows you've never been able to keep it in your pants for very long. Did it once occur to you to try to find some of us? Or even one of us?"

"So you feel I abandoned you," Beowulf said, "and that's your justification for this?"

"Not just this, daddy. I've done so many evil things. If you weighed all the good you've done in your life, against all the terrible things I've done, the world would have been much better off if you'd never existed to create me. I strangled my whore of a mother before I'd even grown a man's hair. She used to tell me so many wonderful stories about you, and your adventures. And every night she'd tell me how you'd come back to her – to us – once your heroic work was completed. Stupid sow. Her name was Aleesa, from Gaul. Do you remember her, father?"

"No."

"Of course not," Dobler said. "Why would you? She's just one among the army of sluts who've opened their legs to you throughout history. For my first hundred years or so, I spent my life tracking them all down, following in my father's footsteps, so to speak. When I found them, I'd give them another taste of the Beowulf family thrust and squirt, before ending their miserable lives. I gave the same service to poor Miss Garrow, while Hellstone held her quiet and helpless for me. Then I watched while Hellstone ripped her to bloody pieces. Oh yeah, I saw her slinking out of your room the other night. I knew you'd been at her, fouling her, like all the others. It's just icing on the cake that you'll be blamed for her murder, while lying on the bottom of the sea. Your reputation will be firmly cemented as the criminal I always knew you to be. Do you know that I used to kill the whelps of your whores too – your other children – until I learned enough about the magic arts to conceive of a better use for them?"

"Their blood," Beowulf said.

"That's right. They've got the same dragon's blood in their veins that we share. I've stashed just over a hundred of your bastards locked away in a secret place, where they are bled every once in a while, to manufacture the fuel that powers Hellstone, and soon his baby brother. I'm building a bigger version of my lovely creation that will be able to hold enough dragon's blood at one time, to generate a level of supernatural power so as to be able to crack the mantle of the Earth with its fist, should I desire it. That's the first project the money I make from my suicide gas will finance."

"Too bad," Beowulf said. "I was going to kill you here and now, so that the world could be rid of you. But now I see that I have to keep you alive at least long enough to make you tell me where my other children are being kept."

"You still think you have a chance to defeat me, old man? Have you been keeping me talking while you try to break those chains? Struggling on to the bitter end? Good for you. Keep fighting the good fight until your last breath is drawn. Too bad though that you've just run out of time. We've been headed out to sea for over two hours now. We should be far enough out to dump you where you'll never be found again."

The false Dobler, Beowulf's son, walked to the back of the compartment, stepping over the hero's prone form, and slapped a large switch near the rear doorway. Immediately the rear door began to lower, with a hum of small motors, whose sound was quickly lost in the fury of cold wind that blew in from the widening hatchway. The temperature in the cabin quickly plunged. For one moment, the dark man stood in the open doorway, holding on to handholds overhead, and shivering in the cold. Then he turned and gingerly made his way back deeper into the compartment. As he stepped once more over his father's body, Beowulf shrugged off his chains, and bolted up off of the deck.

"Did you honestly imagine any number of mundane chains could hold me?" Beowulf said, shouting to be heard over sound of the screaming wind. He grabbed his son around the neck and threw him one-handed to collide in a tangle with the red monster called Hellstone.

While Hellstone struggled to untangle itself from its master, Beowulf walked over to his son's seat and picked up the metal briefcase that contained the suicide gas formulas and bomb prototypes. The straps holding it in place against the bulkhead parted as if they were made of thin paper. With two quick snaps of his thumb and forefinger, he broke off both of the locks holding the briefcase shut. Then, walking back towards the open rear hatchway, Beowulf let all the contents of the case tumble out into space.

"So much for your doomsday weapon," Beowulf said, though no one more than an inch away could possibly have heard him.

Before he could turn back into the cabin, the Hellstone monster collided with him, hitting him low on his back and at an angle, smashing him hard against the helicopter's interior bulkhead, just to the left of the open hatchway. The metal of the bulkhead bowed out grossly with the impact. Control cables and electrical wires, that ran along every exposed surface of the cabin, were snapped, showering Beowulf and Hellstone with sparks. The helicopter suddenly skewed into a violent, shuddering spin. The sudden change in direction spun Hellstone off of Beowulf's body for a brief moment, just long enough for him to grab the creature under each of its arms and lift it with all his might. Supernatural stone met mundane steel and the fragile steel gave way. Hellstone's head tore through the overhead bulkhead, intersecting with the guts of one of the two powerful General Electric turbine engines that drove the aircraft. There was a sudden mind-numbing scream of torn metal, and the crippled helicopter staggered in the air, like a wounded animal.

Beowulf was thrown back towards the still-open rear end of the cabin, which erupted in a blaze of fire. He caught himself on one of the overhead handholds just before he would have fallen out of the craft. Then his body was slammed against the top of the cabin as the helicopter began to plunge in altitude. At the same time the Hellstone creature rushed at him, from out of the fire and smoke in the forward part of the cabin. Hellstone locked its arms around the hero's chest and carried them both out of the aircraft. They fell locked together, spinning and tumbling through the frigid night air, towards the surface of the sea far below. Beowulf had a momentary vision of the wounded helicopter, set against an iron gray sky. It pitched and rolled wildly as its pilots fought to save it and their lives. Then he lost sight of it as they slammed into the sea.

Hellstone was under him as they hit, absorbing most of the punishment of impact, so Beowulf was able – barely – to maintain consciousness. The creature had ceased all independent movement, and had grown extraordinarily heavy, sinking rapidly into the cold seas, taking Beowulf down with it. I guess you finally ran out of gas, Beowulf thought, as he was dragged down into the depths. The hero focused all of his efforts on breaking Hellstone's deathgrip on him. For all of his inhuman strength, it took him more than five full minutes to free himself. He took another 15 minutes to swim to the surface, not by far the longest time he'd been forced to hold his breath.

He broke the surface just in time to see the crippled helicopter finally fail in its struggle to keep aloft. It fell from the sky, a great broken hammer which smashed itself to pieces against the anvil of the sea. Beowulf tread water among the eight-foot troughs and crests of the lurching sea, looking for any sign of life from the wreckage. After an hour he finally accepted what he knew from the first moment – no one could have survived the crash.

At a speed of between 160 to 184 miles per hour, and a range of 578 nautical miles, the Sea Stallion could have been as much as 280 miles from shore. That was assuming his son's plan was to dump him at the aircraft's extreme range and then turn back the way they'd come. If however his son had arranged for inflight refueling, the distance could be considerably greater. Beowulf guessed that he was in the Pacific ocean – only because it was the closest sea to Montana, where he was taken captive – and that they'd have traveled due west out to sea. He took another guess at which direction east lay and started swimming.

Once in his foolhardy youth, he'd swum seven days and seven nights in Europe's freezing northern seas, wearing full battle armor. Even without the encumbrance of armor, this one would likely take much longer. It would be a long, cold swim, no matter how improbably accurate his navigational guesses were.

Chapter Fifteen
Among the Headstones

Beowulf and Doctor Pindahl Valentine watched as workmen fixed the huge marble headstone in place over the grave of Janet Garrow. It was a surprisingly warm early March day outside of Lancaster, Pennsylvania.

"I'm sorry I couldn't be here for her funeral," Beowulf said. He wore a dark gray suit, and his accustomed cap, that had been returned to him – with apologies – from Colonel MacCauley and the Dillon jail authorities.

"You had a good excuse," Valentine said, "being lost at sea and all that. Remind me again where it was that ship finally found you?"

"About thirty miles off the coast of Chirkof Island, in the Bering Sea," Beowulf said.

"That doesn't speak for an overly sophisticated directional sense," Valentine said. As always, he leaned heavily on his cane.

"Give me a break," Beowulf said. "The sky was overcast night and day. I didn't have anything to work with."

"True," Valentine said.

They watched silently together for a time, while the workmen finished anchoring the headstone in place. Once they saw that the job was done properly, Beowulf and Doctor Valentine walked together, away from her grave, towards the black Institute limousine idling quietly nearby.

"You're certain your son was killed in the crash?" Valentine said.

"Reasonably so," Beowulf said. "He was burning the last

time I saw him, and anyone would have died in that crash."

"Anyone normally human," Valentine said. "But I can't help thinking that he was your son, and wondering if you could have survived a similar ordeal."

"There is that," Beowulf said.

They reached the car and climbed, one after another, into the spacious rear compartment.

"We're ready to go," Valentine said to the uniformed driver in the front seat. Then he pushed the button that closed the smoked glass partition between the front and rear compartments. When they were safely protected again from prying ears, Valentine said, "And the Hellstone monster is safely inert at the bottom of the sea?"

"Where he'll stay, unless someone can reach it with about a pint of dragon's blood," Beowulf said. "Not destroyed exactly, but the next best thing at least."

"And finally the suicide gas has been destroyed?"

"Yes," Beowulf said.

"I am satisfied with the outcome of your mission," Valentine said. "Too bad it had to come at such a cost." He looked back once more at Janet Garrow's grave, as the limousine pulled away from it.

The two men rode in silence for a time, each lost in his own private thoughts, watching the headstones pass outside of the car.

"I'll want to spend some time trying to find my other children, in whatever place my son has them locked away," Beowulf said, breaking the silence.

"You'll have the full support of the Institute, in both finances and man-hours, to help you," Valentine said. "Locating a monster making factory, such as he implied, is well within the scope of this Institute's purpose."

"Thank you," Beowulf said.

At the wrought-iron front gates of the Eternal Gardens graveyard, the Institute limousine turned left and entered the traffic, accelerating east towards Philadelphia and other adventures.

Some Acknowledgments and Notes on this Adventure

In addition to thanking the people who helped, this is the part of a book where the author tries to impress his readership by revealing all of the hard work he did researching the story. Those of you who take interest in these behind-the-scenes undertakings can read on. Those of you who don't can skip these pages with nary a regret.

Chapter One

For the record, I didn't write this installment as a cry for help because I've grown despondent over having missed so many deadlines in my career. Any creative writer who doesn't always have a ready cache of at least a dozen new excuses for missing deadlines can hardly call himself a professional.

Chapter Two

I've been carrying my version of Beowulf around with me for many years, long before he showed up in the second and third issues of my Coventry comic books. To me at least he always seemed the perfect pulp adventure hero, and this seemed a good time to finally trot him out as such.

For those of you who prefer your Beowulf in the original furry swordsman version, I can't recommend enough the wonderful new translation of the epic poem by Seamus Heaney, still available in most bookstores, or from

Amazon.com. One of the many things I like about this book is that we get the original Old English and the modern English translation, side by side on facing pages. I once taught myself (a vastly grammatically incorrect version of) Old English to use in a couple of issues of my Elementals comic series (Issues 1 - 3 of the second series), because I needed a foreign language for the inhabitants of a heroic fantasy world to speak. I wanted to reward any reader who'd take the time to translate the odd words, but as far as I know, no one ever did. Struggling through the Old English version of this Beowulf translation is a joy, beyond the fact that it's a great way to waste time I should use in getting more work done.

And as long as we're talking about Beowulf books, if you haven't already done so, pick up the John Gardner novel, Grendel, which retells the Beowulf story (wonderfully) from the monster's point of view. By the way, this isn't the John Gardner who wrote all those James Bond novels, it's the one who wrote Mickelsson's Ghost, The Sunlight Dialogues and far too many other great books.

The first time the Willingham family ever went to a Chinese restaurant (Ruby Chow's in Seattle – where Bruce Lee used to be a waiter at about the same time we used to go there, but I have no particular recollection whether or not he ever served us), my dad wouldn't let us order anything until we'd all mastered the use of chopsticks. We had to pass one of those small restaurant ice cubes from person to person via chopsticks, until said cube had successfully gone twice around the table, without dropping. I should mention that we were a big family. No food until we did it was a great motivator and I've been a deft handler of the things ever since.

Dad was a firm believer in the "throw him in the water and he'll learn to swim" school of instruction. I can still remember a long, lazy afternoon spent sitting out in the middle of a lake, alone in a huge row boat (I was a wee tyke at the time), while dad and my brother cooked an enticing trout lunch in our camp. Every once in a while dad would call out to me that my lunch was getting cold and I really should row back into shore. My fault for asking him to "teach me to row the boat some day."

Of course now days such behavior would be labeled child abuse, which is one of the few reasons I'm glad for being such an old fart (at least compared to my partners in this venture), and went through childhood before such hysterically-overprotective notions took root.

Chapter Four

This is the "how I survived the dragon that killed me" story I've been waiting for years to tell. The dilemma: I didn't want to remove anything from the original Beowulf legend, but still have him around to use in modern stories. This version satisfies both requirements nicely.

Like the city of Pandora, and the state of Coventry, the town of Diversion, and the history behind it, is entirely fictional. But that is indeed the area where Lewis and Clark crossed the Rocky Mountains, on their way out to the Pacific Northwest. Lewis and Clark were often taking side trips away from each other by that part of the expedition, and there is some evidence that – official reports to the contrary – they were no longer sanguine in each others company, and would jump at any excuse to be apart from each other. I chose Clark, rather than Lewis, to discover the good fishing area that became the fictional town, only because Clark's Diversion sounds slightly better than Lewis' Diversion.

James Bama is a real person, and the phenomenal illustrator of the version of the Doc Savage paperbacks, that were published about the same time period as I have Beowulf's comic books being published. He's even better known as a western painter. I kidnapped Mr. Bama into my Coventry world to paint the Beowulf covers, in addition to the Doc Savage covers he produced in the real world. So there.

Chapter Five

I served in the US Army, but for the record, I was never known for being particularly strack.

For this chapter I tried to find how long it took a human body to freeze solid, and then how long, under various conditions, said body would take to thaw again. In both cases I failed to dig up the goods and had to fake it.

Chapter Six

There is a hotel in Seattle called the Edgewater Inn, which is most famous for being built flush with the end of the pier on which it rests, so that hotel guests lucky enough to score a room on the Pacific Ocean (actually Puget Sound, but part of the ocean if anything is) side of the hotel, can fish right out of their rooms. The hotel even rents fishing gear, for those who don't come prepared with their own.

Once, when my dad visited me in Seattle, I installed him in one of those rooms and hardly got to see him the entire visit, because all he wanted to do was fish out of his bedroom – even fishing while in bed. He didn't catch a damned thing, but swore it was one of the best times he'd ever had. Go figure.

I borrowed that one aspect of that Seattle hotel to add a touch of unusual color to my otherwise uninspired but journeyman description of the small tourist town of Diversion. I feel no shame for having done so.

The description of Beowulf's abilities was taken straight out of the original epic poem. The description of the red monster's abilities was forged in a less elegant place.

Chapter Seven

The idea that someone could actually take in enough food fast enough to provide the caloric energy to fuel regeneration, as it was described in this installment, is ridiculous of course. According to a doctor I spoke to, long ago in my Elementals comic book days (when I first played around with the notion of justifying rapid human regeneration by heavy eating), food could not be force-fed into a human being fast enough to provide the calories that would be needed for regeneration, as it's described here.

But if impossible was a good reason not to do something in a story, most of my career never would have happened. Take it for what it's worth.

Chapter Eight

The milky white sap of the Indonesian upas tree was believed so poisonous way back when that its name was an adjective for "malevolent or deadly power" back in the 18th and 19th centuries. According to legend, nothing could live within the vicinity of the deadly tree, and a person coming within even 14 miles of the thing was doomed to die. But, though the sap of the tree is used as a poison, it really isn't so bad as all that.

But this is a story where all legends live, so I've returned the upas to its legendary stature as a magical source of deadly evil. I am indebted to Jeffery Kacirk and his wonderful book,

Forgotten English, for the skinny on the legend of the upas tree.

Chapter Ten

I'm indebted to my friend Matt Sturges, author of <u>Midwinter</u> and <u>Beneath the Skin and Other Stories,</u> for the concept of Immortal's Funk. He didn't come up with it, I did, but he set up the need for such a thing to be created, to explain a problem I had with using Beowulf as my hero for this yarn.

In an unrelated story, Matt used Beowulf as one of the bouncers in a bar frequented by supernatural types – just a nice, throwaway bit of scene decoration, not essential to his story. Having also used a modern version of Beowulf in my own Coventry comic books, with plans to bring him back in these tales, I got to thinking about his cameo appearance in Matt's story. The problem I pondered was this: Why would a famous immortal hero of old be nothing more important than a bouncer in some bar? The answer came with the creation of the concept of Immortal's Funk. Problem solved.

As a bit of serendipity, at about the same time I was coming up with the idea of these moments of needed down time for the big guns of our fictional universe, I learned, through a TV documentary about geniuses, that the man with the highest IQ ever recorded (higher than Einstein, Hawking and all the rest) is currently a bouncer at a New York bar. Okay, fictional immortals and real geniuses aren't the same type of monkey, but I thought it interesting all the same.

Chapter Thirteen

The Sikorsky CH-53 series of helicopters are remarkable machines. In service since the Viet Nam days, it can be outfitted for a number of missions. It is capable of hauling big loads, over long distances, in horrible conditions. The Navy and Marines call their version the Sea Stallion. Us Army boys called ours the Super Jolly Green Giant. In my service days, I often flew in Hueys and Chinooks, but never got to fly in a Sea Stallion, or Green Giant. Damn it.

Other Acknowledgments

In addition to what I've detailed above, I'm indebted to many people who've helped in the creation of this story and the production of this book. First and foremost, I'd like to thank my three partners in the Clockwork Storybook enterprise for their help, so frequent and generous that it would be folly for me to try to list specifics. They are: Chris Roberson, Mark Finn and the afore-mentioned Matt Sturges. Thanks also to Allison Baker, Clockwork's trusty business manager. Gary Groth and Kim Thompson also deserve a pat on the back. They published the first stories set in the Coventry fictional universe. These were in the short-lived comic book series called Coventry.

Shelly Bond, my current (as of this writing) editor at DC/ Vertigo Comics read the first draft of this story, off of a computer screen, in one fevered sitting, staying up late into the night, and showing up tired and miserable the next day at work, to do so. Thanks, Shelly. Your praise, support and critical eye are always appreciated, even though I fail to mention it as often as I should.

This is the first is a series of books that will chronicle the modern adventures of Beowulf, as an agent for the Saint George Group. The next one is called Hyde and Seek and should be available shortly. I also plan to do a number of non-Beowulf novels set in the Coventry world. Two of them,

The Last Fallen Angel and Nevermore are already in progress, and at this moment I couldn't begin to guess which one will be completed and released first.

I love hearing back from my readers, whether it be praise or well-crafted criticism, for this or other stories. If you care to, you can write me in care of the publisher. You can find the Clockwork e-mail address on our publishing website at www.clockworkstorybook.com.

Finally, on the following page, I've added a Beowulf short story to this volume, as an extra treat to those who enjoyed the main story, and just because I felt like it. I hope you enjoy it.

Green Grow the Rushes Oh

This story takes place a little more than a year after the events of The Monster Maker *and shortly after the events of the second Beowulf book,* Hyde and *Seek. It features one of my favorite fairy tale monsters.*

Years ago it had been a lake, but since then had shrunken down to nothing more than a pond at best. Green rushes surrounded its banks. Fat blue bottle flies and tiny gnats and mosquitoes darted and buzzed over its thick, unmoving surface. Its still waters were a deep green with accumulated algae. The stream which had fed it and kept it clean had long since been diverted by land developers – miles away still – but marching implacably into the area, lot by lot. The pond gave off a corrupt smell that hung like a shroud in the dead and heavy Louisiana air. It was an odor of rot and infestation, foul enough to warn all but the most adventuresome or foolhardy creature away – excepting those tiny things that worked in the decay industry, and found there everything to supply their most avaricious desires.

Then one day, with an abrupt crashing of undergrowth, a tall, stocky figure forced his way out of the surrounding forest, through the perimeter of rushes, and down to the water's edge. He wore loose-fitting olive colored safari-style shorts and well-worn brown leather hiking boots over a pair of white socks. He also wore a brown pilot's cap, with a gold wolf's-head pin on its front face, above the brim. His broad chest was bare and his large belly hung over his belt. His naked legs and torso were beaded with sweat.

"Come out, old woman," the man shouted, as he gingerly traversed the pond's shoreline, careful not to actually touch the water's edge. "I know you're down there."

In answer, without so much as a ripple of disturbance, a ghostly figure rose up from the emerald depths, and silently parted the water's surface. Her hair was long and golden, but painted a light green by the tainted lake water. It floated in looping tendrils on the pond's surface. Her eyes were green and her skin was pale and unblemished. Lips like rose-petals slid back from white teeth, forming a perfect smile, which she fixed on the man crouching by the shore.

"Come and swim with me, beautiful man," she said, and her voice was a soft siren's song that tugged at him, almost physically. Her naked arms moved back and forth, just under the surface, languidly treading water.

"Not likely," the man said. "Not in that fetid soup."

"You're mistaken," she answered. "This water is cool and clean." And just like that he saw that he'd been mistaken in his original impression. Everything she said was true. The rippling water was actually clear, shading to sapphire blue in its depths, like virgin alpine ice melt. Below its surface he could see refracted slices of dappled sunlight dance across her round white breasts. "Come swim beside me to cool your body. Let me embrace you to take all of your cares away."

"That's some remarkable trick," the man said. "I was fore-warned about your powers, and thought myself sufficiently prepared for them, but suddenly all I want to do is dive in and have my carnal way with you."

"It's what we both want. Be a husband unto me. Enter my maiden's gate and fill me with yourself. I'll grow strong sons for you in my belly." Her large eyes never left him, proving him the exact center of her universe. Her flushed lips parted slightly.

"Never on the first date, Jenny. I'm not that kind of guy." He found it increasingly hard to breathe in the hot, syrupy air.

"Do we know each other?" A flicker of confusion moved across her features, almost too rapidly to see, before her inviting and seductive expression restored itself.

"Not likely. Very few men who encounter you once live to meet you again." He stood up and paced slowly, back and forth, along the water's edge. Her intent gaze followed him on each iteration.

"How is it then that you know my name? Who are you?"

"My name is Beowulf, and I'm a Licensed Private Hero working for the Saint George Group. My job is to hunt down the world's deadliest monsters, Jenn, and you come in at 37 on my employer's master list."

"How can you call me such a foul name?" She pouted in such a way that he instantly wanted to apologize for every possible slight. He wanted to plunge in, rush to her side and comfort her.

"It's not easy, I admit, with you looking the way you do, and giving off whatever it is that makes me want to throw my life away for the possibility of winning just one of your kisses. But, with civilization finally making its way to this neck of the woods, too many people have recently gone missing near your lair. Think of me as a one-man angry villagers scene, with the requisite torches and pitchforks. No sane community abides a predator in its midst. People are moving in. It's time for you to go, so monsters 38 through 100 can jump up one space each on Doctor Valentine's list."

"Do you imagine you have the strength to destroy me, hero?" She renewed her dazzling smile, and Beowulf felt a red flush of pleasure at its return.

"Not if I jumped in there with you. I'm not dumb enough to try to fight you in your own element – in your place of power. But once I lure you out on dry land I'm told I shouldn't have too much trouble with you."

"But I have no intention of coming out there, and if you continue to resist my invitation to come in here, then we seem to be at an impasse." The sun was almost directly overhead, and the air so muggy it seemed to beat down on Beowulf, standing on the shore, mere steps away from the cool, crystal water.

"You'd think so, but I didn't come alone. Listen closely and you'll hear that my friends with the Army Corps of Engineers have arrived."

"What's that noise?" A more serious look of concern this time.

"The inevitable march of progress," Beowulf said. "Specifically it's the sound of the bulldozer that's busy knocking out a path to us through the trees, even as we speak. When that's done they'll lay down a bunch of those interlocking steel-mesh thingies, they use to make an instant, temporary roadway. Then they'll move the pump-trucks in to drain the pool, and that's all she wrote. What's left of your life can now be measured in a few short hours. Of course you can save them all that work, and save us both the wait, by jumping out here and taking your chances one-on-one with me."

"That I think would be suicide," she said, "and I'm not given to such despair." She floated out further towards the center of the pond.

"There's two good reasons you should do it my way. First, with me you'd at least have a fighting chance, albeit a slight one. Second, I wouldn't have to put up with the inevitable wailing and moaning from some prissy environmentalist puke, upset that I murdered the fragile and sickly Earth, by draining another of our precious wetlands – which is what they make us call swamps these days. Come on, Jenn. Be a sport. Don't make me sweat it out here, for a day or more, just to make sure you don't try to nab any of these guys while they drain your bathtub. Why not go out with a little bit of style? Every monster should end their life with one last glorious battle. Imagine what a better story that would make."

The hero's best arguments failed to sway her, so he sat by the stagnant pool and watched and whiled the hours away. It was twilight before the huge Army bulldozer finally tore away the last line of trees protecting the previously hidden glade. Men in camouflaged fatigues moved heavy generators and large industrial lights, so that work could go in through the night. By dawn the steel mesh roadway had been wrestled into place, and the pump trucks rolled in, belching diesel smoke into the muggy Louisiana air, that had never cooled through the night. All the while Beowulf patrolled the perimeter of the stagnant pond, in case the monster tried to make a run for it.

The three tanker-pump trucks parked well away from the pond's shoreline, outside of the creature's siren influence. Only Beowulf – already having proved himself immune (barely) to her irresistible call – walked the three heavy rubber hoses down to the water – one from the back of each truck. The pumps started with the chugging of huge engines, and the creature's home began to disappear at the impressive rate of 2400 gallons a minute.

The lovely monster pleaded, threatened and bargained with the hero, who ignored her. From time to time she'd attempt to grab one or another of the thick hoses, but she wasn't a terribly quick or agile thing, and Beowulf was always able to pull it out of the water in time. He'd dangle it just out of her reach, attempting to lure her out of the thickening green water. Eventually she'd retreat to curse or sulk and the pumping would continue. The border of her stronghold retracted, inch by inch, requiring that the trucks be repositioned every few hours, to keep their hoses within range.

"You're not much of a hero," she said, "to be afraid of one small girl."

"There's nothing cowardly in avoiding something that would gladly drink my blood and crunch my bones, if I let her. And as perfect as the illusion is, I know what you really are behind that pleasing mask."

After six hours the water had receded enough to reveal the white human bones of her victims, half-buried in the mud of the pond's bottom. Beowulf kept pace with the shrinking shoreline, covered in wet, black mud above his knees. The creature retreated to the last deep pool, where she quietly keened her sorrow.

Work slowed over the final hours, as the trucks had to take turns driving off to empty their tanks, and Beowulf had to spend more and more time unclogging the filters at the end of each hose, as the water turned ever thicker with mud and algae. But twelve hours after it had begun, the pumping stopped, leaving the muddy, grassy glade suddenly quiet for the first time that day. Except for isolated puddles no larger than a foot wide, the pond was gone.

The creature cowered down in the bottom of the emptied hole, curled up in a fetal position, sobbing at the cruelty of her fate. Her illusion of beauty had vanished along with her protecting water. Now Beowulf – and the curious soldiers standing around the edge of the great hole – could see her for what she really was. She was a withered old crone, whose age-spotted skin was gouged with a thousand deep wrines and their ten thousand tributary wrinkles. Each of her joints were horribly swollen. Her hands and feet were grotesque webbed things, each finger and toe ending with a long yellow claw. Her hair was gray and filthy, her nose a hooked beak, and her eyes were dead obsidian things, set under a protruding proto-human brow. Her teeth were sharp fangs, of varying length, set haphazardly into her jaws at random angles. They were colored the same deep green as the vanished water.

Beowulf approached her with difficulty, each foot sinking deep into the mud with each step. When he couldn't maneuver around them, he would gently move the human bones out of his path, disrupting them as little as possible. They'd be needed over the next days – or weeks – for victim identification. The rancid smell got worse, the closer he came to her. When he reached the creature, he bent down and quickly twisted her head around and around, until it came off of her body with a single dry snap.

Later that night, in his Baton Rouge hotel room, he killed two bottles of single-malt Irish whiskey, while taking an hours-long bath – constantly replacing the near unbearably hot water – until he felt clean again.

To order the three issues of Coventry the comic book series, you can go online to the publisher's website at: www.fantagraphics.com or call them toll-free at 1-800 657-1100.

The price per issue is $3.95 plus a $1.00 shipping fee. However, if you order all three issues they'll throw in the shipping for free.

Printed in the United States
780800002B

9 780970 484185